A HOME IN THE WEST

OR

EMIGRATION AND ITS CONSEQUENCES

M. Emilia Rockwell

EDITED BY

Sharon E. Wood

UNIVERSITY OF IOWA PRESS, IOWA CITY

Originally published in 1858 by the
Dubuque Express and Herald
Copyright © 2005 by the University of Iowa Press
University of Iowa Press, Iowa City 52242
http://www.uiowa.edu/uiowapress

Printed on acid-free paper
Design by Aaron Cruse
Printed in the United States of America

Library of Congress Cataloging-in-Publication Data
Rockwell, M. Emilia (Mary Emilia), b. 1835 or 1836.
A home in the West, or Emigration and its consequences /
by M. Emilia Rockwell; edited by Sharon E. Wood.
p.   cm.—(A bur oak book).
Includes bibliographical references.
ISBN 0-87745-943-6 (pbk.)
1. Women immigrants—Fiction.   2. Women pioneers—Fiction.
3. Married women—Fiction.   4. Iowa—Fiction.
I. Title: Home in the West.   II. Title: Emigration and its consequences.
III. Wood, Sharon E.   IV. Title.   V. Series.
PS2723.R63 H66 2005
813′.3—dc22   2004062114

05 06 07 08 09 P 5 4 3 2 1

Photo of Lansing, Iowa, from the Paul C. Juhl Collection,
State Historical Society of Iowa, Iowa City

INTRODUCTION

by Sharon E. Wood

When printers at the *Dubuque Express and Herald* peeled the freshly inked pages of *A Home in the West, or, Emigration and Its Consequences* from their press, they surely never imagined it would endure to find readers in another century. The pamphlet they stitched and trimmed in 1858 was an object for immediate consumption, an emigration tract designed to recruit easterners to settle in the Upper Mississippi Valley. Priced at ten cents, it hardly seemed the stuff of literature or history. Yet even as they bundled the little books for distribution, they may have recognized that this tract was different. Written by a young schoolteacher, *A Home in the West* directed its persuasions at an audience of women, using the form of the domestic novel, a genre popular with women readers. What took shape under those printers' deft hands was almost certainly the first original novel published in Iowa and probably the earliest to portray life in Iowa as well. In twenty-three pages of tiny, cramped type, it told the story of a young couple who left Connecticut for the village of Newburg, Iowa, where they found friendships and hardships and finally success. The story was conventional, but the booklet was not. Emigration tracts directed specifically at women are rare, and one in the form of a novel is unique. For readers today, *A Home in the West* opens a window on the concerns and experiences of women in the mid nineteenth century and offers a fresh view of the "pioneer" generations of white Americans who settled Iowa and the Midwest.

. . .

M. Emilia Rockwell was just twenty-two and a newcomer to Iowa when she published her novel. Born Mary Wells in Elmira, New York, she grew up along the border of western New York and Pennsylvania. Like her heroine, Annie Judson, Wells married a carpenter, and the couple emigrated to Iowa after their 1856 wedding. Norton and Mary Rockwell made their home in the Mississippi riverport village of Lansing, about ten miles south of the Minnesota border.

The fictional Newburg is not Lansing, nor is Annie Judson an alter ego of Mary Rockwell. Instead, Rockwell's knowledge of Lansing and Dubuque informed her depiction of Newburg, just as her observations of the social and economic upheavals of the 1850s taught her about the concerns of women whose families were considering emigration. Historians studying the diaries and letters of westering women have found that they were often reluctant migrants, loath to leave kinfolk behind and overwhelmed by the increase in labor that women sometimes faced. But private concerns were not the only ones that might deter emigrants. The first years of Mary Rockwell's marriage were also years of violence and upheaval in the West, and Rockwell's novel sought to reassure readers that eastern Iowa, at least, was a peaceful and prosperous place.

Hard Times and Boom Towns

Although set primarily in Iowa, *A Home in the West* is also a novel about the disruptive effects of industrialization in the East. With her opening sentences,

4

Mary Rockwell invoked the separation of "home" from "work" created by the new economic order, and she offered the hope that women, as caretakers of the home, could temper the alienation and destructive competition of an industrial economy. Outside the Judsons' cottage, all is storm and bluster; inside all is "peace and comfort." Even Annie Judson's name suggests her role. The real Ann Judson was one of the most famous women of the antebellum era. The first American woman to go as a missionary to foreign lands, Judson wrote a pious memoir, defended her husband when he was imprisoned by Burmese authorities, and died a martyr. "Annie" Judson is not called upon for such courage or such sacrifices, but she is the moral center of the novel, guiding her husband Walter's choices and, like a missionary, bringing "refining, softening influences" to the "money-seeking, speculative" West.

The values embodied by Walter and Annie Judson stand in stark contrast to those that jeopardized their peace and security in the industrial East. Rockwell wrote with nostalgia about apprenticeship, a labor system that was disappearing by the 1850s. In its ideal expression, apprenticeship bound a boy and his master together in a surrogate child-parent relationship. The apprentice lived in his master's household, cared for and taught by both his master and his master's wife. As production moved out of workshops and into factories, and as unskilled laborers replaced skilled craftsmen, the apprentice system broke down—a change that was more than evident by the time Rockwell wrote. Nevertheless, Rockwell invoked the apprentice system to criticize the heartless and impersonal wage labor system that replaced it. Orphaned as an infant and spurned by his aunt, Walter Judson learned carpentry, "social graces," and "purity of taste" in the household of his master, Mr. Ethnolds. The ties that bound Walter to Mr. and Mrs. Ethnolds were intimate, infused with the warmth of family. In contrast, the men for whom the adult Walter worked felt no compunction about cheating him of his wages. Hard work seemed to yield only more debt, a cycle Walter proposed to escape by moving west. When disaster struck again in Iowa, the moral clarity of Annie's vision persuades Walter that he must pay his own workers even if it means a temporary setback for his dreams.

The problem of unpaid labor and unpaid bills would have been familiar to many readers in 1858. The previous winter, the collapse of a major financial

6

company and a series of related disasters led to the Panic of 1857, pushing the country deep into a recession—the second in three years. When Rockwell paused to address "Sir Millionaire," whose business failed as "hundreds of thousands went down in the ruin," she had in mind the five thousand businesses that went bankrupt in the aftermath of the 1857 panic. Stephen C. Foster's classic song "Hard Times," published in 1854, became an anthem for the decade.

In real life, the recession struck hard in the Mississippi Valley, but in fictional Newburg, the drive to build a new town ensures that Walter finds plentiful work. Rockwell's depiction of Newburg, lying in a cosy little valley between towering bluffs, fit Lansing as well. Like Newburg, Lansing was a new and booming town. Platted in 1851, just three years later the town already had 440 residents. By 1860, it had grown to nearly 1,200. Such rapid expansion fueled construction, and carpenters like Norton Rockwell found ready work. So did young, literate women like Mary Rockwell. She worked as a schoolteacher in Lansing, as did her sister-in-law, Lydia Rockwell. Indeed, several of Norton's siblings left Pennsylvania for Lansing, echoing one theme of

A Home in the West, that family ties could be restored and strengthened by migration.

The connection between town growth and carpentry work helps explain why Mary Rockwell chose to write an emigration tract. As long as emigrants poured into Lansing, demand for new housing, new shops, new mills, and new public buildings would continue. Especially for those who settled in urban places like Lansing, the influx of new settlers—whether farmers who relied on the town's port, or town folk who provided shops and services—assured the prosperity of those already there. Mary Rockwell's domestic novel promoted her economic interests by encouraging others to follow in her footsteps.

Labors of Love

Like most young women of her day, Mary Rockwell worked for pay. She earned money as a schoolteacher, and she may have earned something for writing *A Home in the West* as well. Young women in the 1850s commonly found employment as household help or in mills and factories, but they usually left their jobs at marriage to take up the unpaid labor of homemaking. That Mary Rockwell held a job after her marriage suggests either that Norton Rockwell's employment in Lansing was not as steady as Walter Judson's in Newburg, or that Lansing had a shortage of qualified teachers, or perhaps simply that Mary enjoyed teaching. Whatever her reasons, Mary Rockwell was relatively free to work because she had no children.

For most women, household labor combined with child care was a full-time job. Indeed, it was often more than full-time. So many girls and young women found employment as household help because the labor required to "keep house" for a family was more than one woman could manage. The kinds of work required to feed, clothe, and maintain the health of a family had changed only a little in the years between 1800 and 1858, but the way they were portrayed in popular culture—in marriage manuals, advice books, and domestic novels—had changed a great deal. Increasingly, writers were reluctant to admit that homemaking involved work at all. "Work" was what men did outside the home; what happened within the home was "love." "Work" earned pay, but the labors of love performed by women at home remained outside the cash economy. Indeed, home was redefined in this era: what was once a place of economic activity became a refuge from industrial capitalism.

The newly married Mary Rockwell embraced this ideal of women's role in the home—even though she herself worked outside the home for pay. Her novel is filled with references to women's productive household labor, yet she chose to celebrate above all the "unuseful arts": the geniality, grace, and taste that a wife should embody in spite of hours spent at hard, heavy work. Walter and Annie Judson's visits with "queenly" Bertha Newcome illustrate the way Rockwell rendered women's labor all but invisible.

At the Judsons' first visit to the Newcome home, Bertha served her guests tea—"nice preserved berries, . . . fresh bread and sweet butter, plain cake and dried venison." Its simplicity was meant to contrast with the fashionable life Bertha had left behind and to suggest the virtues of life on an Iowa farm. Yet the menu contains within it the evidence of Bertha's labor: hours spent picking and cleaning the berries, then boiling them into preserves on a wood-fired stove—probably on a hot summer day. The stove itself must be stoked with fuel and its temperature regulated by the skill of the cook, who must also rake out its ashes daily, clean up the spilled and burnt preserves, and black the stove regularly to prevent rust. All this Bertha must accomplish with a four-year-old boy and twin girls to care for and keep safe from the searing heat of the stove. And this produces only the preserves. Bertha also tends and milks dairy cows, separates cream, churns butter, makes bread and cake, and processes deer meat into dried venison. (Please, let someone else do the butchering!) While some additional labor is suggested during the visit—Bertha weaves rugs, scrubs floors, and washes dishes—other work goes unacknowledged. With a family of five, she must spend hours every week hauling and heating water and scrubbing clothes (using soap she makes herself from saved fat, ashes kept from the stove, and lye). Twins in diapers would only increase the burden. Yet Bertha still finds time to do fine needlework to "grace the table and walls" of her home and, later, to home school her children. And all the while she remains "radiant with health and beauty."

In rendering invisible the labor that created the ideal home, Rockwell endorsed the new gender ideal that accompanied industrialization. Men and women were to occupy "separate spheres." Men's sphere was work, money, and the world. Women's sphere was culture, love, and the home. Though Annie presumably shops for her family, she does not know how much they owe the grocer. Food preparation is an act of love that she does not contaminate with the sordid concerns of commerce. Moving to Iowa becomes a way for the Judsons to restore the proper balance between home and work, to protect the home's status as a refuge from labor and competition. To be a refuge, it must not admit the labor that creates it. Rockwell promised her readers that on the Iowa prairie, life could be refined and cultured, women could retain their beauty, and opportunity for all could bring families together (in contrast to the greed that split Walter's family apart).

The News from the West

Rockwell answered women's private fears by depicting ideal marriages and families reunited on the prairies, but she also purposefully addressed some more public concerns her readers might have harbored. For those back east contemplating migration, the news from the West was disturbing. In the months before Rockwell published her novel, Indian massacres, conflicts with the Mormons, and the Dred Scott decision tempered the enthusiasm for migration. Potential settlers feared violence and worried that the expansion of slavery would thwart the aspirations of white settlers for fair wages and secure futures. Directly or indirectly, Rockwell's novel responded to each of these issues, reassuring her readers that Iowa remained a haven for white settlers, not a place of discord or danger.

The biggest news to come out of Iowa in 1857 was the killing of thirty-three settlers in northwest Iowa by a band of Wahpekute Dakotas, who also took three women and a teenage girl captive. Eastern newspapers quickly dubbed the episode the Spirit Lake Massacre and reported the gruesome scenes at isolated cabins. When three Wahpeton Dakotas successfully ransomed the youngest captive, Abigail Gardner, and returned her to Fort Snelling three months after her capture, the orphan became a sympathetic public figure. The army officer assigned to escort Gardner back to Iowa, Lorenzo P. Lee, interviewed her about her experiences and published his *History of the Spirit Lake Massacre!* later that year.

Lee's presentation of the Gardner family history (which he spells Gardiner) oddly parallels Rockwell's portrayal of the Judsons. Gardner's father was a factory hand in western New York touched by "Western Fever" who "felt sure that he might do better elsewhere." To Lee, Gardner's decision to go west was a fateful error. If only he had been satisfied to stay in the East, "the war-whoop of the Indian would never have echoed through his peaceful cottage, the scalping knife never would have horrified his children and sent them and their beloved parents to an untimely grave in the wilderness." Lee's history, published in Connecticut, surely shaped the way Easterners viewed Iowa—even though Spirit Lake was almost 270 miles from the Mississippi Valley.

With the story of the massacre fresh in the minds of readers, Mary Rockwell may have felt she could not avoid the subject. She addressed it by staging an encounter between Annie Judson and a group of Indians so benign they proclaim their readiness to cede the land to whites and go west, where the sun sleeps (an image which suggests extinction as much as relocation). Through Annie's voice, Rockwell assured her readers that if the Indians were "dangerous or troublesome they would not be allowed to encamp so near the town." In fact, Indians were probably regular visitors to Lansing in the 1850s. The region comprising Allamakee County had been shared by diverse Indian populations, including Dakota, Ojibwa, Meskwakie, and Winnebago, among others. Although most had been forced further west, some Indian settlements persisted in southern Minnesota and in nearby Clayton County, Iowa.

Rockwell's depiction of the Indian visitors to Newburg, however, betrays more familiarity with white stereotypes than with Indian cultures. Focusing on work, Rockwell illuminated the contrast between gendered activities among Indians and those accepted by whites. Among the Indians, the women are "busy about the fires," cooking meat and corn. They also make baskets and engage in trade. The men sit or lie about, they have time to talk, and they have no ambition to learn reading or writing or to adopt white ways. As Annie sees them, the Indians reverse white expectations that men's work should be visible and women's work obscured— underscoring Rockwell's point that the Indians are less civilized and thus undeserving of the land. Annie's visit concludes with a note of humor. Walter teases her about her absence: "I feared you were taken by the Indians." "I was not, but Freddy was," Annie replies. Their joke depends on their certainty that Indians are no danger, but it comes only months after the conclusion of a real Indian captivity story.

The Mormon War

Spirit Lake was not the only massacre reported in 1857. That September, Mormon militiamen and civilians, aided by Indians, murdered a group of emigrants traveling to California. Of 140 or so women, men, and children from Missouri and Arkansas, attackers killed all but 18 small children. The massacre at Mountain Meadows in southern Utah came just as the U.S. Army was advancing on Mormon territory. Although shocking in its scale, it was not the first example of Mormon violence that year. During the same weeks that stories of the Spirit Lake Massacre made their way east from Iowa, newspapers reported the murder of apostate Mormon William Parrish and his son by true believers determined to silence critics of the church.

By 1857, hostility between Mormons and federal authorities had reached the brink of civil war, but the conflict had come on gradually. After an Illinois mob murdered Mormon prophet Joseph Smith in 1844, Brigham Young led one group of followers to the shore of the Great Salt Lake. Over the next decade, thousands of converts followed, many following the Mormon Trail across southern Iowa. In 1850, President Millard Fillmore acknowledged Young's leadership of the growing settlement in Utah by appointing him governor of the territory. But relations between the federal government and the Mormons quickly deteriorated after 1852, when the church publicly acknowledged the practice of polygyny, or plural marriage. Most Americans were horrified at what they considered the immorality of "Mormon harems" or polygamy. Young's practice of governing Utah as a theocracy only made matters more difficult. Increasingly, Young pursued a separatist path, defying federal authority and encouraging his followers to isolate themselves from those they called "gentiles"—non-Mormons—who attempted to settle or travel in the territory.

The "Mormon War" found its way into *A Home in the West* through the story of a group of immigrants from Europe bound for Utah. As in her portrayal of Indians, Rockwell's depiction of Mormons owes more to popular prejudice than to actual Mormon belief and practice—but it also reveals what most Americans, especially women, found so disturbing about polygyny. To Mormons, marriage modeled on that of the biblical patriarchs was a religious obligation revealed by God. Only a minority of church members embraced it—though by 1857, the numbers were rising. Mormon women who defended plural marriage argued that it was preferable to monogamy because, in a world where godly women outnumbered godly men, it helped ensure that every woman could find a good husband. To Rockwell and the readers she addressed, plural marriage threatened to reduce women to slavery. No longer endowed with a special sphere as queen of her home, woman would also forfeit her claim to moral authority. Each wife replaced in her husband's affections by a younger woman would become a common drudge, and the natural order of respect for aged mothers would be turned upside down.

Ironically, both Rockwell and those who embraced the new religion were grappling with the changes brought about by industrialization. For Brigham

Young and those who followed him, patriarchal marriage and an isolated, agrarian colony in the basin of the Great Salt Lake allowed them to escape—at least for a while—the social and economic consequences of the industrial era. Men who were patriarchs in their homes would not be wage-slaves in mills or mines. Rockwell's view of modernization was more ambivalent. She accepted the new ideal of separate spheres but also hoped that the Midwest would prove a moderating influence. "All the works of man—the steam mills, the factories and warehouses—could not mar or destroy the beauty of those hills that guarded Newburg," she wrote. Nature defied monopoly: "'Thus far shalt thou go and no farther' was written by her pen upon the rocky bluffs." To the men who were drawn to the Mormon faith because it promised to return their status and authority, Rockwell offered an alternative. "Stay here and become laborers until you are able to become possessors of farms of your own," she urged. "Stay and become a colony of freemen in the land of a free government." The Jeffersonian ideal of the yeoman farmer lived on in Iowa.

A Place for Whites Only

In the call to the immigrants to become "freemen," Rockwell quietly raised the greatest political issue of her day. As an overt theme, the question of black slavery is nowhere in *A Home in the West*. Among the diverse population of Newburg, the reader finds Germans, Irish, Norwegians, Welsh, Swedes, French, Indians, and Yankees—but no African Americans and no Southerners. Yet the question of slavery shaped the way Rockwell's audience considered migration to the West. By 1858, the civil war in "Bleeding Kansas" had temporarily slowed, but the Dred Scott decision had changed dramatically the meaning of race and slavery in Iowa and other free states bordering the South.

In early March, 1857, Supreme Court Chief Justice Roger B. Taney delivered a decision that denied the right of either Congress or territorial legislatures to ban slavery in the territories of the United States. His opinion also implicitly upheld the right of slave owners to carry their human property anywhere in the country, including into free states like Iowa. The decision was a victory for proslavery

Southerners but left other Americans uneasy—even those who had no wish to abolish slavery in the South. Mary Rockwell was silent about her own politics, but the historical record contains hints of her views. Her publisher, the *Dubuque Express and Herald*, advertised itself as "pledged to uphold the doctrine of Popular Sovereignty," a reference to the view that voters of each state should decide whether or not to admit slavery. In addition, Norton Rockwell was a Democrat, meaning he belonged to the party of most slave owners and most men who supported popular sovereignty. If Mary Rockwell's politics reflected those of the men around her, she almost certainly supported popular sovereignty as well.

Under the Missouri Compromise of 1820, Iowa and other territories north of Missouri were closed to slavery, but that did not mean they were open to free blacks. Like other states in the Old Northwest and the northern portions of the Louisiana Purchase, Iowa placed restrictions on black emigration and on black participation as citizens. African American settlers, for example, had to post bond when they entered the state, to guarantee that they would not become burdensome paupers. They were also barred from testifying against whites in court. Such restrictions were meant to preserve the state as a place for whites only, where white workers would not have to compete with African Americans. Because employers paid lower wages to blacks, white workers resented them as rivals whose low pay jeopardized whites' ability to win fair wages. Slavery was even more objectionable to white wage workers, who could not hope to compete with workers who earned nothing at all. This fear of competition led many white Americans to support preserving slavery in the South, anxious that liberty would unleash millions of competitors. Yet they also opposed the expansion of slavery into the West. The boundless opportunities of the West—the good wages and plentiful jobs that built the Judsons' home and reunited Annie's family—would vanish if black slaves became the carpenters and farmers of Iowa.

Although Mary Rockwell remained silent about black slavery in America, she used the word "slave" repeatedly in *A Home in the West*. For her, "slavery" was associated not with blacks in Missouri and Arkansas but with Mormon immigrants in Iowa. Yet her use of the word suggests a consciousness of the antislavery arguments that had come to dominate women's political debates about slavery. For

Rockwell, Mormons made "slaves" of their daughters, and they were bound by "shackles" and "fetters." To antislavery women, Mormon polygynists and southern slave owners were comparable patriarchs, debauched men who rejected monogamy and abused their power over women. When the church elders selected new wives among young converts, they perverted marriage in much the same way that slave owners debased their families by forcing bondwomen to become concubines. Rockwell may have supported the doctrine of popular sovereignty, and she may have portrayed an Iowa reserved for whites only, but she echoed in her language the arguments of antislavery women.

A Different Kind of Future

In 1858, Mary Rockwell imagined a future in which a carpenter-husband became a wealthy town proprietor, and a family reunited to grow old and prosperous together on the prairie. Nothing could have been further from the truth of her own life. By the early 1860s, Norton and Mary Rockwell had grown discontented with life in Lansing. For reasons

that remain unclear, they left Iowa and moved to
Providence, Rhode Island, where Norton sold insur-
ance. In 1870, Mary gave birth to their only child,
Martha Corinne, and two years later the family
moved once again, this time to Manhattan. Both
Norton and Mary found employment at the New
York House of Refuge, the oldest juvenile reformatory in the country. Even though she had a toddler
to care for, Mary taught in the institution's school.
Norton drew on his carpentry skills in the manual
training department. Their experience at the New
York House of Refuge opened a new era in their lives
as they chose to devote themselves to working with
delinquent children.

After about two years at the House of Refuge,
Norton and Mary Rockwell became administrators,
taking over the Connecticut Industrial School for
Girls. Norton became superintendent, Mary assistant superintendent. This was a common arrangement for all kinds of residential institutions in the
late nineteenth century. Ideally, a married couple
would suffuse an institution with the qualities of a
home and provide a model of companionate marriage for the residents. To the chagrin of the school's
board of directors, the Rockwells failed on both

counts. Although the details are obscured by time, Norton Rockwell apparently fell in love with Ada Sheppey, a schoolteacher who had worked with Mary at the House of Refuge, and who had come to Connecticut with them to teach at the Industrial School. In 1877, the board of directors replaced the Rockwells with a new superintendent couple—though Mary remained an employee of the home, listed in the 1879 annual report as a "visiting agent." A history of the school published in 1881 made no mention of Norton Rockwell's affiliation with the institution but praised Mary for her service "under circumstances of great difficulty." The Rockwells divorced, and Norton Rockwell married Ada Sheppey about 1879.

The woman who had once written romantically about a wife's duty to submit to her husband now found herself divorced with a young daughter to support. Drawing on her experiences in New York and Connecticut, Mary Rockwell found a position as superintendent of the Milwaukee Industrial School, a reformatory for boys and girls established in 1875. Returning to the Upper Midwest, Rockwell used her job to reunite her own family, creating a home for herself, her daughter, her widowed mother, and an uncle—not in a cottage on the prairie but at an urban school. In 1881, the school hired a steward to supervise the building and grounds. Their choice, Dewey Austin Cobb, had been a teacher at a reform school in Providence, Rhode Island, through most of the 1860s and 1870s. His selection for the job in Milwaukee hints at a longer acquaintance with Mary Rockwell. She and Norton had lived in Providence during the time Cobb worked there. It is plausible that Mary Rockwell's first involvement in juvenile corrections dated to that period, and she and Cobb may have first met at the Providence school. Whether their acquaintance began in Rhode Island or in Wisconsin, it soon grew beyond mere employment or friendship. In 1882, Mary Rockwell and Dewey Cobb married.

They remained in charge of the Milwaukee school until 1886, when the Wisconsin legislature voted to establish a new institution that would have drawn away most of the clients of the Milwaukee school. Frustrated with their prospects in Wisconsin, Mary Rockwell Cobb and Dewey Cobb resigned and moved to Philadelphia, where they took charge of the Foulke and Long School for Girls, an orphanage and boarding home. There they remained until at least

1910, with Mary's daughter Corinne sometimes teaching at the school. Dewey Cobb died in 1915. The date of Mary's death remains unclear but came sometime between 1910 and 1920.

. . .

After publishing *A Home in the West*, M. Emilia Rockwell Cobb never published another work of fiction. Instead, she wrote a number of articles for professional journals about working with children. Her daughter Martha Corinne, however, embraced a career as a writer. Under the name Corinne Rockwell Swain, she published dozens of poems and essays and several plays for children. During the 1920s and 1930s, she was a regular contributor to the *Saturday Evening Post*.

This new edition of *A Home in the West* brings Mary Rockwell's novel to a new audience of readers. Punctuation has been modernized and obvious typographical errors silently corrected. In most cases, original spellings have been retained.

Selected Bibliography

Bagley, Will. *Blood of the Prophets: Brigham Young and the Massacre at Mountain Meadows*. Norman: University of Oklahoma Press, 2002.

Boydston, Jeanne. *Home and Work: Housework, Wages, and the Ideology of Labor in the Early Republic*. New York: Oxford University Press, 1990.

Dykstra, Robert R. *Bright Radical Star: Black Freedom and White Supremacy on the Hawkeye Frontier*. Cambridge, Mass.: Harvard University Press, 1993.

Gordon, Sarah Barringer. *The Mormon Question: Polygamy and Constitutional Conflict in Nineteenth-Century America*. Chapel Hill: University of North Carolina Press, 2002.

Johnson, Paul E., and Sean Wilentz. *The Kingdom of Matthias: A Story of Sex and Salvation in Nineteenth-Century America*. New York: Oxford University Press, 1994.

Lee, Lorenzo P. *History of the Spirit Lake Massacre! 8th March, 1857, and of Miss Abigail Gardiner's Three Month's Captivity among the Indians. According to Her Own Account*. New Britain, Conn.: L. P. Lee, 1857.

Rockwell, M. Emilia. *A Home in the West, or, Emigration and Its Consequences*. Dubuque: Express and Herald Office, 1858.

Roediger, David R. *The Wages of Whiteness: Race and the Making of the American Working Class*. London: Verso, 1991.

Schlissel, Lillian. *Women's Diaries of the Westward Journey*. New York: Schocken Books, 1982.

Stampp, Kenneth M. *America in 1857: A Nation on the Brink*. New York: Oxford University Press, 1990.

A HOME IN THE WEST

CHAPTER I

The resolution.

The humble home of a mechanic in a pleasant village of Connecticut, is the opening scene of our story. In its cheerful kitchen, with its neat rag carpet, glowing coal fire and white curtains, sat Annie Judson awaiting the return of her husband to the evening meal. It was nearly six by the busy little clock upon the mantel, and though a blustering March storm was raging without, all within the little dwelling indicated peace and comfort. In a pretty willow cradle slept a baby boy of six months in his pure night clothes, while the mother sat busy with sewing by his side in a neat calico dress and plain collar. The supper was upon the table, if we except the closely covered dishes by the fire, and the tea-pot into which the water is poured from the steaming kettle, as a familiar step is heard upon the gravel walk.

"You are late to night, Walter," was the greeting of the young wife as she sprang to open the door into the entry and met a snowy form just within it and received a hasty kiss upon her fair brow. Assisting him to remove his overcoat and hat she took them to the door, shook the accumulated flakes from them, and quietly hung them away.

Walter had sunk into a chair near the stove, and buried his face in his hands. With no word of comment or inquiry, Annie brought from a closet his slippers and drawing a stool to his feet, playfully attempted to remove the heavy boots. Thus aroused, he drew off his boots and donned the slippers, made some remark about the weather, asked "what have you been doing to-day?" and going to the cradle, kissed the baby, *waking* it of course, for what *man* ever kissed a sleeping babe without waking it? Annie left the room for some milk and on returning found him in the same despondent posture as at first. A sadder look came over her face, as she fed the babe and returned it to the cradle. Then gently approaching him she said softly:

"Supper is ready, Walter."

"I do not wish any to-night," he replied without raising his head.

"But you will eat with me, now that I have waited so long for you. Come," she added playfully, "I will not hear one word of your troubles till after tea, and if anything is wrong I know you want me to cheer you up."

It was even so; and already had the process of "cheering up" commenced. There was no withstanding her gentle manner and pleasant voice, and he sat down at the little table, and as she poured his tea and filled his plate, ate almost as heartily as usual of the plain, but well-cooked food. Before the close of the meal, he seemed almost to have regained his usual good spirits.

"And now," said Annie as she again seated herself at his feet, "you must tell me what is the matter."

"There is little to tell, Annie," he replied, the gloom settling back upon his brow. "I have seen Benson to-day, and he refuses to pay me for that last job, as there is an informality in the contract which allows him to do so legally, though he knows that it is my just due, and even with it, I would have lost upon his work."

"How much is the amount?"

"Eighty–five dollars, which with my losses on Warren's house and shop, make one hundred and fifty lost within six months. Wages are low, and I am now in debt with no means of paying since this has failed me."

"How much do we owe at the grocery store," again asked Annie.

"About thirty dollars, and as much more in small bills for shoes, clothing, and wood. What to do I do not know. I have no work engaged before the middle of April, and then have to wait six months for my pay. A pretty state of things." He went on bitterly, "a poor man is compelled to run in debt because he must wait for his dues, and then often to be cheated out of it at the end. Now instead of having money to pay these bills and something over towards getting a home, as I expected, I can collect barely enough to pay the rent for the next quarter, and keep us in provisions for a few weeks."

Annie was silent. The case was worse than she had anticipated, and she looked in vain for any suggestion which would relieve his anxiety.

After a pause, Mr. Judson went on. "There is one thing I have thought of a great deal lately, Annie, though I hardly dared propose it so long as I saw any other hope. If we could go to the West, to one of those new States where work is plenty, wages high and land cheap, we could make a more comfortable living, and besides soon have a home of our own. It is no place for a poor mechanic here—work is scarce, competition raging so high as to keep wages at starving rates, and no one is willing to pay cash to a mechanic, though he is expected to give money for all he purchases. In those rich farming lands of the west, provisions are cheap, while the wants of the emigrants keep mechanical labor in great demand, and farmers receiving money for their produce, are prepared to pay for necessary buildings and furniture in cash. Now Annie, is not this the best thing we can do? In fact my mind is and has been settled for some time, and nothing but opposition from you will keep me here. I have tried it long enough; we have been married two years; I have worked hard, we have lived plainly and had good health, yet are now worse off than at first. We certainly can expect nothing better in the future, and why starve in this teeming, crowded eastern world, when there are homes and wealth for us in the beautiful, boundless West?

"What do you say, darling," tenderly lifting her to his lap, and seating her there, "shall we go?"

What could Annie Judson say? Walter's statements were correct; he was honest, sober, industrious and economical, yet was now, and was likely to be, in pecuniary difficulty. In his present location he could hope for little improvement in his circumstances; so he turned his eyes, as many a poor man has done before and since, longingly toward the West.

"The West,"—that land of promise brighter than Canaan to the desert wanderers! What dreams of happiness, wealth and fame cluster around the very name! It is to many the realm of enchantment; every effort there is crowned with success, every hope produces in gold fruition peace and plenty! Do these dreams remain unbroken? Do the hope-buds bursting from scarred and stunted branches in the populous olden lands, open in rich and splendid joy-flowers when transplanted to the wide expanse of waving prairie and towering bluff; of shining rivers and rich unfailing earth treasures? We shall see.

Possessing firm reliance upon the judgment and discretion of the husband, Annie would have shrunk at any time from opposition to his purposes, though she was ever a counsellor and confidant in all his plans and transactions. She now felt more than usually fearful of exerting an enormous influence. She saw that disappointment and embarrassment

had already shaken his confidence and courage—
that he could no longer "labor in hope," and she
feared the result upon his mind and habits should
such experience be repeated. So overcoming all
weakness, and strong in her love for her husband,
she strove to look hopefully upon the picture he
drew of a prosperous future in the distant West.
Then they passed to plans for the arrangement of
their affairs. The money intended for rent and
household expenses would pay the grocer's account,
and perhaps a part of the others. The sale of their
furniture would cancel the remainder of their debts
and furnish funds for the journey, with a small
balance for first expenses in their new home.

Thus they conversed long after retiring, and
Walter Judson slept that night a happier man than
he had been for weeks. He had not dared to hope
that his young wife would so readily leave her
parents, brothers and sisters, to whom she was tenderly attached, and the large circle of friends and
relatives around them. He remembered, as sleep was
closing his eyes, that she had not once spoken of this
sacrifice. He did not know that, waiting until he was
sleeping, she softly left his side and, resuming her
dress, sat for long hours in the room they had left,

while tears that had been suppressed in his presence, flowed freely down her cheeks. She thought of her kind, indulgent father, her gentle mother, her two noble young brothers, and the young sister, the pet of the household. Memory went back to her childhood; she thought of all their love and kindness, their tender solicitude for her welfare, and remembered that to them Walter was comparatively a stranger. Even in her first grief, she felt more for them than for herself.

It had been a fond hope, and often spoken of between herself and her mother, that they might ever remain near each other; and this was the first sudden intimation of disappointment.

Annie had been a *woman* through all that long evening, with all a woman's devotion and self-denial; now she was but a *child* with all a child's abandon of grief at parting with her earliest friends.

But there came a calmer feeling. She knew that her feet were in a path of *duty*, and her heart grew stronger. She thought of the vows so lately spoken; yet needed not the sense of duty to bring to her lips the words, "whither thou goest, I will go." The bitterness of the struggle was over. Annie Judson sank upon her knees, and fervently prayed for the occupants of the home she was leaving and for a blessing upon her own little home circle, which was now truly to be "all the world to her." Then strengthened and refreshed, she returned to her pillow, and pressing her lips to her sleeping husband's cheek, and encircling the babe with her arms, she was soon sleeping calmly beside them.

CHAPTER II

Preparation.—The Journey.

The arrangement for removal went on rapidly for as
Walter had intimated, it was not a sudden impulse,
but a fixed determination to which the consent and
approval of Annie had removed the last barrier, that
had found expression on that desponding evening.
He had no near relatives of his own, and his wife and
baby Fred, comprised his world. Though he wondered at Annie's calmness and felt grateful for her
readiness to acquiesce in his judgment, it is probable he could know little of the extent of her
self-denial. He was again hopeful, almost extrava-
gantly cheerful, and she would not quench the new
light in his eye, to avoid all the suffering of leaving
her friends. Of the home circle she had been almost
a worshipped member. The eldest child of parents
in comfortable though not affluent circumstances,
she had been carefully educated, and possessed from
childhood an amiable, lovely disposition and strong

clear judgment. When at the age of twenty, her father gave her in marriage to Walter Judson, he trusted she would be to him a blessing and aid in all the pursuits of life. And nobly did she resolve to redeem the trust reposed in her.

Walter was worthy of a loving, devoted wife. Though his sphere in life might be styled humble, he had nobly resolved to attain in heart and mind the loftiest standard, and had in leisure hours and moments gained much scientific and classical knowledge, and was a deep and earnest thinker. Left an orphan in infancy, he had been taken to the home of a wealthy maiden aunt in Massachusetts, and during childhood moved among the scenes of his father's early life. But the ancient spinster was changeable and capricious in her moods, and suspicious lest Walter should regard anything as rightfully his own upon the premises; and at length in a fit of ill-humor, she sent him away from the old homestead at the age of fourteen years, lest he might expect her to make him her heir.—Perhaps the recollection that his father had been induced, while very young, to sign away his claims upon the estate to herself and an elder brother, in consideration of a few hundreds which he very much needed, was an uncomfortable one; at least Walter found a happier home with Mr. Ethnolds, a carpenter in the village near by, and with whom he served an apprenticeship at his trade, than he had ever known in the house of his only known relative. And in the pleasant, cheering influence of a genial household circle were developed those kindly, social graces of spirit which looked out from his earnest eyes, while to the superior education and accomplishments of Mrs. Ethnolds, he owed his love of literature and his purity of taste—his lofty standard and inflexible allegiance to all that is true and beautiful in our being.

They were sleeping in the church yard now, those friends of his boyhood, and their deaths had sundered the last links that bound Walter Judson, our hopeful young emigrant, to the world outside his own family, with any great degree of tenacity. With Annie beside him, and his boy to win name and wealth for, he should be at home anywhere.

Two weeks from the night on which we first made their acquaintance found our young adventurers with all arrangements completed and the place of destination selected.

From the sale of their furniture one hundred and seventy-five dollars remained after all debts were canceled. Of this, seventy–five would suffice for traveling expenses and freight upon the few effects they had resolved to take with them, leaving one hundred for the purchase of some simple furniture, rent of rooms, and purchase of provision, until a permanent situation could be obtained. It seemed little to depend upon in a land of strangers, yet to Walter's hopeful spirit all was bright. He had no fears—no misgivings—once in the West, success would be certain. If not expressed in words, this was the spirit of his dreams.

It was Saturday night, and the following Monday would witness their departure. Annie's family had refrained from any word of discouragement, and at the hour of twilight they all sat, speaking now and then cheerfully of the future, but with a sadness weighing upon every heart as they thought of the coming separation.

"My children," said Mr. Hastings (Annie's father), as he turned toward them, "you are leaving us, yet I cannot feel that you are to be given up. I shall feel as if you were yet among us, when I remember that the same Father will watch over you everywhere, the same Providence preside over your footsteps. Trust in him, my children, and we shall always feel that you are his and he will make you ours again in his own good time."

And the hale, genial man of fifty years looked 'round upon his family with a tenderness and pride pardonable in one who had striven as he had to render them just what their youthful promise began to indicate they would be.

The heart of the mother was growing too full, and Annie seeing the tears upon her cheeks, called with forced cheerfulness to her young sister, a sweet, sunny haired, blue eyed girl of fourteen summers, to come and sing Freddy to sleep. Then they all sang together as the clear girlish voice commenced the familiar air of "Old Hundred," to the words:

Give thanks to God, he reigns above,
Kind are his thoughts, his name is love.

The full, deep base of the father, united with that of the eldest son Henry, while Edward added a rich tenor at the second line, and Annie a sweet, pure alto. The mother listened, and as the christian's faith triumphed over all earthly sorrows, her heart grew calmer, and she thought how sweet it would be to hear those voices joined in singing the eternal praises of their Redeemer in Heaven.

The Sabbath found them for the last time in the family pew at church. For the last time they listened to the voice of the pastor who had married Annie's parents, baptized herself, and lately given her in marriage to one who had one won her pure young heart. Walter's face was thoughtful and solemn—he had just begun to realize the strength of the ties they were breaking. But no faltering appeared in Annie's calm demeanor, no cloud came over the clear light of her eyes. She had prayed for strength to enable her to meet the duties of this day, and it was given.

The day came to an end—the Sabbath School class was given up to her successor—the last visit and blessing of her aged pastor and his wife, were received, and at family prayer her father had read with his voice trembling with suppressed feeling, "Let not your heart be troubled, ye believe in God, believe also in me," and had committed his dear ones to the care of Him who "doeth all things well." They retired early, for sunrise must see them upon their journey.

We will not linger at the little Depot to hear the farewells spoken there upon that bright spring morning. The first beams of the sun touched Annie's waving handkerchief as it disappeared from the car window, but not before the mother had accepted the brightness of the banner as an omen of the future.

They were gone. And the family no longer fearing to pain the hearts of the departing ones by giving way to manifestations of grief, returned to their home to feel for the first time the vacancy made in their midst by Annie's bridal.

Walter's hopefulness and buoyancy returned as the cars rapidly bore them westward; and Annie, too, soon recovered composure as she smiled upon her babe as he lay looking wonderingly at his new surroundings. The journey was a pleasant one, and gladly would we linger with them to admire the many lovely features of our land seen in the tour from Connecticut, the land of hardy thrift and close economy, through the broad Empire State, and westward from thence through the fair new sisterhood of States, Ohio, Indiana, and Illinois, till they reach the beautiful thriving young cities upon the banks of the "Father of Waters." But a few reflections of the journey will suffice. As they proceeded westward, they found the cars crowded with emigrants. Others than themselves were seeking a new home.

Annie sat looking about her as the shadows began to fall on the second day of their journey, and ventured a thought of all the homes bereft of loved ones, of all the hearts left desolate in the eastern land between which and themselves they were fast placing mountains, vallies, prairies and rivers. But the theme was too sad, and she turned her thoughts to the hopes which were swelling in the hearts of that company of wanderers. Why had they left their homes to seek new scenes and cares? What anticipations nerved them to dare the unknown realities of a new, untried mode of life? What did they all hope for? And then her thoughts turned inwardly, and she questioned, "what do I hope for in this new life?" And her heart gave back the answer, "For courage and strength to nerve our hearts, for room and opportunity to become what soul and mind demand, for a home where all shall be our own, for soil which has never yet felt the tread of guilty extortioners, and above all for the blessing of God upon our endeavors." And as she gazed out upon the broad expanse of prairie waving with its first spring blooms, and thought of the welcome its broad acres had in store for their new occupants, she felt that enlargement of spirit we all have felt as we breathed for the first time the pure air of the new world: the influx of great thoughts, of enlarged sympathies, and widening hopes and purposes. The night of the fourth day saw them safely roomed at the hotel in the village which had been their destination. And here we will leave them till the morning.

CHAPTER III

Fair Prospects—Indians—A Sad Story.

A pleasant little village in Iowa—Newburg by name—was the anticipated residence of Judson. Though its location dated but three years into the past, it was fast becoming a beautiful and desirable situation for settlers of all pursuits in life. Neat cottages and tasteful yards and gardens were daily increasing, many of them owned by men who had never before possessed homes. Walter noted many evidences of thrift and successful enterprise, and that upon almost every face there was a look of hopeful energy; and the joyous contagion spread to his own heart. It was as if a new life had been given him. The darkness, care and disappointment of the past were all forgotten in the anticipation of future success. Certainly Newburg was very unlike the slumberous, quiet villages at the east of its own size, for the constant influx of emigration kept up the most lively, business-like air imaginable.

Work was plenty, and Walter was soon engaged at good wages by a carpenter who had contracted for a large amount of work. A small house was rented, some plain furniture bought, and soon they were once more settled at housekeeping, and with fair prospects for the future. Hope made those prospects almost certainties, and their first letters home contained glowing, but not really exaggerated, accounts of their new and beautiful home.

It was a quiet, balmy afternoon in May. The wild flowers were blooming in profusion on every spot of unoccupied ground, and birds and bees were busy among them. Annie, with little Fred in her arms, strolled out of the precincts of the little village towards the green, flower-gemmed prairie. Scarcely out of sight of home, she came in view of two wigwams or Indian huts. Fires were burning before them, and some squaws and Indian children were busy about the fires, while near by several men were sitting or lying upon the ground, with all the appearance of stoical indifference so peculiar to the race. Annie started with surprise, and turned to retrace her steps. Then remembering that if dangerous or troublesome they would not be allowed to encamp so near the town, she turned back in curiosity, and resolved to visit them. She had never before seen an Indian, but fear was no part of her nature. So with the babe in her arms she walked up to the group around the first fire. The eldest squaw looked up with a smile—it was not unusual for the whites to visit them out of curiosity.

"White squaw want basket?" she said, producing some of beautiful workmanship. Annie admired them, purchased one of the smallest for Master Fred's amusement, and essayed to converse with them. "Indian live here always?" she asked, trying to imitate the style of their sentences.

"No, come down the river in canoe last night;—got fish, duck, berry, basket for pale face. Indian want blanket, tobacco, money."

She spoke in her own language to the other women, and they soon surrounded her with their articles of merchandise. "I do not want to buy, I came to talk," said Annie.

"John Shango, he talk. Squaw, she work: cook meat and corn. Talk to Shango," and she pointed to a tall, middle-aged Indian on the ground. He rose to a sitting posture and looked at Annie quietly for some time.

"Give white papoose to me," he said, reaching for the babe.

Annie hesitated a moment, and then placed her boy in his arms. His fair, soft skin, blue eyes and pretty embroidered dress, contrasted strangely with the dark-skinned, fierce looking red man.

"Pretty boy; got big eye. Pale face papoose very nice. Grow up big; be great man, know long word; talk paper talk. Indian papoose know nothing; no good; fish, hunt, make basket. White papoose all good; get all Indian have."

"The Indian papoose must learn long words and paper talk and be like white man," said Annie.

"No, no," and he shook his head emphatically. "White man house too big—school too many. White man want land. Red man go 'way West. The sun is our father. We go where he sleeps."

Twilight was coming on, and Annie held out her arms for the babe. He gave it to her, and rising walked by her side a few paces, then returned to his couch upon the ground. Annie hastened homeward in the deepening shadows, and met Walter just within the village. "I feared you were taken by the Indians," he said playfully, taking his child from her arms. "I was not, but Freddy was," she answered, and related her visit to the wigwams.

In a small building near Mr. Judson's residence lived a sober, honest-looking Hibernian with his wife and three little ones. Outside the back part of the house, a flight of stairs led to a little room above which seemed to be solely occupied by a fair, slender-looking young girl of seemingly some sixteen years. At the little window in the end of the room, she sat all day long stitching silently with a shadow ever upon her white brow, and an anxious wistful look in her dark blue eyes. Annie's favorite window was opposite that of the young seamstress, and as she saw her sitting there daily with the same untiring industry, the same clouded, saddening look, she wondered why she was there alone, and what had made her young life so joyless.—Once she looked down and smiled as little Fred, sitting beside his mamma at the window, crowed and threw up his hands in baby admiration of the pretty scarlet cloth of his new frock. Annie returned the smile with one so warm and pitying that the young girl's heart seemed to receive a glow of sunshine into its gloom.

The next morning as Annie was busily "putting to rights" her little kitchen, a timid rap at the door was heard, and she opened it to admit her interesting young neighbor.

Annie greeted her warmly, and gave her a chair. She was a little lonely in her new home even with Walter and baby, and gladly welcomed her visitor.

"I came in to inquire," she said in a low, sweet voice, "if you have sewing to hire done, and would be willing to give me work."

Annie was very sorry, but her family was small, and she never hired any sewing. She had excellent health, and preferred to do all she could herself. The young girl bowed, and rose to go. But Annie begged her to sit a while with her, adding "you must be lonely at home, are you all alone there, or have you some one with you who is ill?"

"I am alone," she replied; "I thank you for your interest. I will tell you why I who am so young am living alone among strangers, and you will not wonder that I do. But perhaps it will not interest," she added hastily. Her words betrayed a foreign accent.

"I shall be very glad to hear it," said Annie, and the young lady went on.

"I am from France, and my parents are now living there, my young brothers and sisters with them in our beautiful home. One year and a half ago I was sixteen years of age, and on my birthday I was married to my father's ward who had always lived with us. His name was Gerald Lefay. We had loved each other from childhood, and when he was coming to America, and wished me to marry him before he started, my father who could deny him nothing, gave his consent with the understanding that I was to remain at home for one year till he had prepared a home for my reception. But at the end of six months Gerald wrote that a family of his friends were to leave France for New York immediately, and urging me to come with them to that city where he would meet me. I plead for and obtained my parent's consent to do so. But on arriving at New York we could hear no tidings of him. I remained there a month.—He did not come—his friends went to New Orleans to reside, and I seeing his name in a Western paper as the purchaser of some land in Iowa, spent my last money in hastening to this place. But it was not he who bought the land—it was located by the old Frenchman who lately died here, in that name however, and I still hope that it was by his direction and that he will come himself sometime, if he is living, to claim it. In that hope I remain here supporting myself by my needle, and finding a home in the little room over the residence of Dennis Riley. His wife lived at the house where I boarded in New York, and is my only acquaintance here. I have had sewing from a tailor here until this week, when I found he had no more to give me, and being obliged to seek it elsewhere, your kind face at the window yesterday made me resolve to come first to you."

The village, now city, of Newburg demands our passing notice and description. Let us look upon it as it appeared to Walter and Annie from a slight eminence, to which they strolled on one glorious June morning.

CHAPTER IV

The beautiful, widening river, its waters lying smooth and glassy beneath a cloudless sky, flowed between high banks of novel beauty.—Between these "bluffs" lay the most cosy little vallies, stretching back until they met the wooded hills beyond, whose tops formed the beginning of free and boundless prairies; at the foot of the eminence on which they stood, lay the village, bearing everywhere the signs of its hurried growth, yet abounding in the evidences of future beauty and prosperity. In many of the streets the native flowers and berries were still growing, while at the distance of a few rods almost princely dwellings were in progress of erection. Much of the air of the unbroken wilderness lingered there still, yet the sound of hammers, the rattle of omnibuses, the hurrying footsteps of the great city were there also. It was a strange, yet pleasant medley of art and nature. But the loveliness and inspiration of such a view cannot be imagined or imprisoned in word; only one who has stood upon one of those green carpeted bluffs in the morning freshness, has felt that swelling tide of inspired life flowing through the whole being at the realization of the truth that God has given to the burdened sons of toil in the olden States, this vast and supremely beautiful land as their own. It must be a hard heart, which does not rise up in thankfulness to "our Father" in such a place.

The arrival of new comers, though of almost daily occurrence at Newburg, was still a matter of intense interest to its inhabitants. Annie had anticipated much loneliness and want of society, but few weeks had elapsed ere she found herself introduced to a circle of acquaintance even larger than at home. There was a warmth of greeting, a frank, earnest welcome in their manner, for which she had not been prepared and for which she could not account, until she remembered that each one had also lately left dear ones and home behind; and experience had taught them the feelings of the stranger in a strange land. Here, too, were refined and accomplished ladies—even the fashionably delicate and fastidious among them—wonderfully reconciled to the trials

and hardships of living in small rooms with plain
furniture and all of the privations of a new settlement, with the prospect before them of elegant
residences and boundless wealth, when the wilderness about them should be made to blossom as the
rose; true, there were here no such hardships as the
agricultural emigrant experiences upon his "claim"
far from civilized society—no fear or loneliness—
only the deprivation of the refinements and luxuries
of aristocratic life. And perhaps they were learning
lessons which would make them better and happier
when once more surrounded by their lost privileges.
It might be so.

Walter, with his first glances at his new associ-
ates, had penetrated the shrewd, calculating, yet
ardent character upon which the rapidity of Western
improvement so much depends.

And still they came. Every boat that traversed the
winding river was laden with adventurers. Young
men of energy and courage, too eager to wait the
slower conveyances of the older country to wealth
and honor; men of broken fortunes and saddened
hearts; speculators already rich with Western gains;
and farmers seeking homes upon the beautiful
prairie land, which presented in one year from the

time of occupation the appearance of the oldest cultivated fields of the East.

All the strangeness, hurry and buoyancy of intercourse, produced an excitement unknown amid the conventionalities of older society.—Hearts seemed larger and more generous; not that the material beauty of the loveliest spot can change human nature: selfishness was still shrewd and cool; but there was room here for all—no man need build upon his neighbor's downfall—and so hands were grasped heartily, and warm welcomes spoken, as one after another came to share the toils and gains of the Great West. And yet, may it not be, that the blooming, ever changing tinted prairies, the oak-crowned hills, the free magnificence of waters, the pure freshness of the air, constantly reminding of the lavish generosity of nature, had some effect upon the soul?

The first of October, six months from his arrival, saw Walter the possessor of two hundred dollars in cash, and an engagement of work for the winter, which would prove an ample support for his family. And their thoughts began to turn toward the *home* they had so long hoped for; and Annie's day visions were of vine draped porches, of rose bushes and shrubbery all their own. Of a little white fenced yard, where Freddy, now beginning to try his own powers of locomotion, might play without danger. They were beginning to look with interest at unoccupied lots, and to think of the selection of one, when Walter came home from work one evening with newer plans.

"What do you think, Annie, of putting off getting a home here a little longer, and laying out what funds we have in government land?" he asked.

"What can *we* do with government land?" laughed his wife. "I hope you are not turning speculator."

"No, not exactly, but there is a beautiful tract of land, I am told, some fifty miles west, upon the Des Moines river, the most desirable in the State, and I have been thinking it might be a good investment to purchase what I can at one dollar and a quarter per acre, and wait until another year for a home here."

The proposal impressed Annie favorably, notwithstanding it was a death-blow for the present to the dreams of flowers, vegetables and a neat white cottage she had been indulging. But she had seen and heard enough during their short Western residence, of the profits made upon investments in land, to feel that such a course might be much the best for them to pursue. So after a three days' journey upon horseback to view the region, for he would not be content with the testimony of others, Walter returned the owner of one hundred and sixty acres of new land in the valley of the Des Moines. Back to his labor he went cheerily, willing to wait the lapse of time to prove whether his had been a wise choice.

Letters passed frequently between the parted sisters, for the blue eyed Mary became the amanuensis of the household. Only when Annie plead for a few words direct from her father and mother, came sometimes a sheet filled with their kindly council and loving messages. The parting was not a bitter one though its beginning had been so sad, for the letters from the absent ones were ever filled with hope, and chronicles of success and pleasure at all they met in the new world around them. So that dear home circle felt that it was far better so, than to have them among the old scenes again, with saddened hearts and disappointed hopes. Then would they be truly lost, when toil without full reward, and the crushing, disheartening disappointment so often attendant upon effort where the laborers are more plenty than the fields for labor, had bowed down, and at last crushed out the nobler part of life.

All things which spring up quickly were rivalled by the growth of the young city of Newburg. The changes wrought in that one bright summer of golden sunshine, purple mists and gorgeous prairie blossoms, were almost incredible. Building materials could scarcely be furnished in sufficient quantities: though that difficulty seemed likely soon to be overcome as two rival steam saw mills were just commencing their labors near the site of the village. Fine looking stores were erected, a noble stone Court House completed, and the principal streets began to assume the appearance of wealth and splendor as well as thrift and industry.

And so the bright, glorious autumn days came and passed. Serene and cloudless skies hung over prairie, river, bluff and valley; every few days brought changing hues to the waving prairies, now they were gorgeous with scarlet blossoms, now softened into delicate blue and purple, then flashing out again in golden and orange flowers, and anon rich with full crimson tints. It was glorious at the sunset hour to be out alone in the midst of boundless varying loveliness, and be free to dream, reflect and breathe in life and health of body and liberty of soul from the wandering winds.

Then when the frosts of the late November nights had robbed the waving grass of life, how the prairie fires flashed upon the skies their fitful brilliancy!

They were a sight full of splendor and novelty to all who had never yet spent this season in the prairie-land. The rushing, flaming tongues of fire, flashing and glowing as they preyed upon the deadened vegetation; the swiftness of the advancing flames as they sped from their starting point all over the level race ground; the frightened animals fleeing to the waters for safety; all this constituted one of the grandest, most splendid sights on earth. Not all of Art's devices could arouse in the mind such grandeur of thought, such wild leaping of heart and soul into the arena of life's action. Turning from that gorgeous, fiery conflict, one longs thus to consume the deadened blooms and faded hopes of the past, and like the flame to speed onward ever in brightness and splendor, till,—as the river quenches the prairie fires,—the waters of death roll before us, and upon the solemn shore the fire of soul goes out forever, or leaps to Heaven with exultant strength.

CHAPTER V

The first snow storm came, and winter set in "for earnest" early in December. The river was frozen over, and the daily mail by steamboat was exchanged for a weekly one by stage. All communication with the world around was cut off, except by sleighs to the nearest rail road depot. And then speculators and residents of Newburg began to turn their attention from city improvements and land speculations to projects for rail roads which would connect them with the east during all the year. It was not probable that many winters would pass ere some of the speculations which filled their brains would be realized. Still all was favorable with our young emigrants, the Judsons. Health and prosperity seemed determined to smile upon them, however they might desert others.

That there were discontented repining hearts in Newburg, was however, a fact soon ascertained by

Annie in her intercourse with her neighbors. It was
not unusual to hear the most grievous lamentations
over the trials and sorrows of Western life. Yet she
had sufficient acquaintance with human nature to
feel assured that most of the speakers would have
been "grumblers" anywhere: belonging to that class
to whom the chief pleasure of life consists in firmly
believing and impressing upon others that they have
suffered, toiled and endured far more than any
others. True, there was to many much serious
difficulty and real care and hardship connected with
their removal westward—But perhaps an equal
number of families who had never moved from the
limits of their native townships, might have to
recount an equal number of serious illnesses, sad
accidents, and losses by fire and water. We are so apt
to consider all that happens to us during or after a
certain act of change as a consequence of that
change, forgetting that no situation can exempt us
from the mutations appointed by a wise Providence
to attend all earthly things.

Swiftly the winter days passed by, notwithstanding the dread of loneliness and discomfort that had
oppressed many hearts. There were social parties,
sleighing parties and evening visits in abundance,

and these were attended and enjoyed by all. Even
the aristocracy of Newburg, for there was an aristocracy, though its limits were not very clearly
defined, joined with zeal and enjoyment in the pleasures of social intercourse with their lately unknown
neighbors. If there is any place where one learns to
prize others for what they are really worth as social
intelligent beings, aside from all advantage of
wealth or station, it is in the social gatherings of a
new settlement. No one can know what have been
the antecedents of any other, and the most arrant
pretensions to former wealth, respectability and
education, are not noticed except they are accompanied by the mind, heart and manners indicative of
such exaltation. Society is formed anew and upon a
truer basis. The few butterflies of fashion who have
with unsoiled wings survived the flight from their
former abodes, will, it is true, congregate together,
forming a "set" of their own stamp. But aside from
these, the really earnest, thoughtful seekers of the
good and beautiful in spiritual and social as well as
physical nature, are being magnetically attracted
and discovering congenial and sympathetic tastes
and pursuits. The possession or want of wealth is of
little weight where all are placed in the light of

adventurers, and the present fitness of a person for companionship is considered, rather than what his parents' standing might have been, or of how many thousands they might have been possessed. Thus sympathetic friendships spring up quickly where a likeness of feeling is perceived, for there is little of the false measurement so common in old, aristocratic circles. Perhaps many a refined and exclusive family might open their eyes in unaffected wonder, could they see the daily associations and new social relations of their western relatives, yet we believe that not one of those who have thrown off the trammels of conventionality and sought companionship and friendship with a sole regard to what should be its basis and support, has ever become less truly refined in taste or manner, while the nobility of character and humanity of soul has been increased.

Three churches had been erected in Newburg, a Methodist, a Baptist and a Presbyterian. Each was usually well attended, and embraced a goodly number of communicants. The pastors of the two latter were settled among them, while the Methodist pulpit was supplied by a minister from the neighboring town Wawkena, distant some fifteen miles. Sabbath schools were held in each, Bible classes instituted, prayer meeting kept up, and Christians belonging to either of the three readily found a home and a cordial welcome as an assistant in the labors of their brethren. Walter and Annie had both become members of the Presbyterian church near their eastern home soon after their marriage, and the prospect of a home among those of their own faith was not among the least of their pleasant anticipations of a home in Newburg. Three months from their arrival had seen them admitted by letter into the church in that place. True, Annie's first Sabbath at church had filled her heart with sad thoughts and longing to behold the Sabbath gathering in the dear old church at home. She thought of the gray haired pastor whose tremulous tones had so often blessed her there and of the family pew where were now sitting the group from her father's cottage.

She knew they were thinking of her as they gathered there and saw her vacant seat, and the first tears she had wept since leaving them sprang to her eyes as she looked around upon that sea of strange faces, and realized that between her and that dear familiar church, lay many hundreds of miles. The pastor was a young man,—earnest, zealous and eloquent in his master's cause. Scarcely had the tones of the hymn died away on that first morning at church, when, in a clear, full voice, he announced the text—"Casting all your care upon him; for he careth for you." And in the contemplation of the full love and tender care of a heavenly parent, Annie's heart was comforted, and her spirit renewed for the trials and duties of life.

"I believe *you* find yourselves at home in the church here?" remarked an intelligent neighbor as they together returned from church. "Well, there are many who do not. Probably there are as many professing Christians in Newburg who belong to sects not yet able to be represented here, as there are in the churches. But their number is growing less, for the want of church standing and religious society is so much felt, that sectarian prejudices on all sides are yielding, and they feel willing to unite with Christians of other names rather than stand alone.

"And, in my opinion," he continued, "this is one of the good effects of western emigration, for our old prejudices get broken down, and we are not so strenuous about trifles of difference."

We will let a letter from Annie to her sister Mary give some account of their feelings, hopes and circumstances at the close of the winter to which we alluded in the beginning of the present chapter.

"At home to-night, dear sister, you are singing our old familiar evening hymns. Well, Walter and I have been singing too, and have sung Freddy to sleep, and I have laid him in his little bed, (he has never had a cradle here) and left him sleeping there while I write to his 'auntie,' whom he may never know. He is beginning to talk a great deal, and Walter tells him about 'grandpa, grandma, and uncle and auntie,' every day. One month more and it will be a year since we left old Connecticut. You will not feel jealous if I say it has been a short, bright year to me. Walter is very well settled in business here, and really doing very well. You already know that he is the owner of one hundred and sixty acres of land on the Des Moines river. But that is of no present use to us. He has earned this winter only about twenty dollars per month over all expenses, but that we think is pretty well for winter wages. Next summer, we hope to buy a nice lot, large enough for a house and garden, and to commence building the house. So in one year more we shall be living in our own house, and be able to raise our own vegetables. You would think our hopes and plans very moderate and humble, could you know of the magnificent air castles many here are constantly building. But we are very happy to have even this prospect before us and sometimes we extend our plans so far as to dream that at some time, if brother Edward continues to be partial to a farmer's life, we may have you all, father, mother, Henry, Edward and you, settled upon our land in a nice, pleasant house, with a parlor just like ours at home and mother's chair at the window, with the stand with the Bible and knitting work upon it, just as it stands now at the window of our dear, dear home. And this new home would be only fifty miles from us!"

CHAPTER VI

"A note for you, Annie," said Walter, as he sat down to dinner one day, producing from his pocket a delicate white envelope, addressed in a pretty hand to "Mrs. Walter Judson."

"Ah, an invitation to take tea this afternoon with the lady I met at Mr. Wilmot's, and was so much pleased with—Mrs. Waltham. And my acceptance will of course depend upon yours, for 'Mr. Judson will of course come to tea,' is the closing line."

"And I *will* go 'of course,' for I am half in love with your new friend, from your description, and anxious to see her—so fix Freddy up and I will take him when I go to the shop, and bring him in at three o'clock. I suppose that is the hour you ladies congregate for tea-drinking; isn't it?"

Mrs. Waltham, who was now visiting at the house of her sister-in-law, Mrs. Wilmot, was really a most agreeable and instructive companion. Her age was about forty years,—the last fifteen of which had been spent among the scenes of the far west. Many a story of pioneer life could she relate; many a journey had she taken on horseback with her husband, over the broad prairies to the nearest settlement to their cabin home. Eight years of the time she had she resided ten miles from any other settlers, and surrounded by Indians and wild beasts. Yet nothing in her manner indicated the rough, illiterate character which people of the east so frequently connect with the idea of the western pioneer.—Her mind was not only well cultivated and stored with a more than ordinary amount of useful knowledge, but her manners were graceful, her language well chosen, and singularly pure and correct. Later years had brought emigrants to their retreat, and their lonely farm was now a populous village, and Mr. Waltham the wealthy proprietor. Their family of three sons and two daughters had received their English education from their parents, and been sent by turns to a flourishing academy in an adjoining State, to pursue languages and scientific studies, and now would not unfavorably compare with the scions of the proudest eastern families.

The afternoon visit at Mrs. Wilmot's passed in the recital of many peculiarities and interesting circumstances connected with their new homes, yet perhaps nothing was more interesting than the description by Mrs. Waltham of the Mormon emigration, which she had witnessed the preceding summer—Walthampton, their residence, lying upon the direct route to Utah. We give it in her own words, only omitting the occasional remarks and queries of her interested hearers:

"During the month of August the emigration from Europe began to come in—companies from one to three hundred passing almost weekly. Those who possessed wealth had carriages for their families and wagons filled with goods, while the poor traveled on foot. Each man drew a small hand-cart, in which he was permitted to carry only thirty pounds of baggage. Each cart was followed by from two to five women, who assisted its locomotion by pushing.— The youngest children were sometimes placed in the carts. Those whom I noticed most particularly were some companies from Wales, who stopped at our village for several days, hiring houses for the most wealthy, and providing encampments for the poor foot travelers. If any among the young girls of these poorer families attracted the notice of the elders or richer Mormons in the wagons, they were provided with seats and rode with their admirers, though none of them were permitted to become the husbands of any more 'spiritual wives' until their arrival in the promised land. Thus some young, blooming and healthy girls rode during the entire journey, while their mothers, old, sickly and fatigued by long travel, and with young children in their arms, and by their side walked painfully day after day. These girls were the promised 'spiritual wives' of the elders they accompanied.

"One of them, after having vainly begged to exchange places with her aged mother during the journey, on reaching Walthampton resolved to leave them and remain among strangers, rather than submit to the fate before her. Several ladies became interested in her, and provided a place where she might live in a small family and learn the language. Yet during the stay of the Mormons in the village, she remained among them in order to be with parents, brothers and sisters as long as possible.

"The Elder to whom she was promised, had stopped some fifty miles back, and arrived in Walthampton on Sabbath morning following the

Thursday on which they encamped. On learning her determination, by report from the Mormons, he became furious with passion, and threatened her life should she refuse to go on. One of the ladies, who spoke the Welsh tongue, saw him hurrying by, and instantly guessed his identity and errand. Hurrying to the encampment, she was just in time to listen to a volley of execrations, reproaches and threats of the most awful import addressed to the young girl who sat weeping bitterly. He paid no attention to the lady's entrance: but continued his angry tirade, heaping upon her the most dreadful curses, and bitter sarcasms, evidently not dreaming that a word was understood by the intruder. The lady listened silently for a few moments, then turned to him and uttered a few words in Welsh. He turned pale, gazed at her stupidly, and without a word more, walked quickly away out of sight.

"Turning to the girl the lady advised her to gather her clothing quickly and return with her. This lady was of Welsh descent, and had already gained much influence among them. While waiting for Mary's preparations, she addressed the Mormons, several families of whom were around them. 'Why do you go on?' she demanded. 'This journey is wasting all your effects, killing your wives and little ones, making slaves of your daughters. You will find the "promised land" but a scene of discord and crime. You are misled—duped—destroyed by the emissaries of this sinful people. I too, am a native of Wales—I cannot see my brethren and sisters so sacrificed. Remain here in our fair Iowa. You have perhaps lost nothing by the exchange from the mines of Wales to these rich farming lands. Stay here and become laborers until you are able to become possessors of farms of your own. Cast off the fetters of fear—fear of these vile men who have deceived you. Stay and become a colony of freemen in the land of a free government rather than the enemies of that government.' Two men came forward as she paused, and stood before her; their wives and children came and stood beside them—the wives of their youth—not the promised spiritual wives who had followed them across the seas. 'We will stay,' they said firmly. 'The faith of Mormon is not what they told us when they lured us from our homes. We have suffered, and should have died ere now but for the kindness of the gentiles among whom we were traveling. We are no longer Mormons—we will become Americans!' And the two families commenced preparations to leave the camp, and before night were safe in the homes of friends. 'And will you too stay?' demanded the lady turning to the others. But the men shook their heads in silent refusal, the women wept loudly and despairingly. They dared not throw off the yoke which made them the slaves of their spiritual advisers whose disciples and converts they were.

"As Mary and her protectress left the camp, a woman followed them weeping. The lady stopped and spoke kindly to her, 'Will *you* stay with us?' she said. 'No,' said the poor woman—'my husband left me in bed with my babe one week old and with another woman started for America and Utah. I found where he had gone and got up, took my babe and followed in the next vessel. I overtook them in New York. My husband dare not cast me off, and I have since traveled in company with him and that woman. I shall never give him up—I shall not live long—I know that I am dying, but never while I live will I leave them one moment'; and she turned and rejoined them.

"The next morning the Mormon camp was broken up, and the poor deluded, suffering emigrants recommenced their march."

"And what became of those who stayed?" asked Annie.

"The two men got work as farm laborers—built small shanties for their families, which soon assumed the appearances of comfortable cabins. They are now getting comfortable livings, and laying up money to purchase farms. The girl Mary was married a few weeks since to a fine young Irishman with a good farm, and is now one of the happiest wives in Iowa."

CHAPTER VII

"Oh, Walter," exclaimed Annie, looking up from a letter she was perusing, a letter from home,—the next week after the visit at Mr. Wilmot's. "You remember Bertha Lester, don't you? Well, she is living only twenty miles from us in the same county. She married a merchant you recollect,—Arthur Newcome, I think his name was,—and went to live in Providence. He was wealthy then, but Mary writes that they have heard that he failed two years ago, and they came West and bought a farm with the little they had, and are now living in Westville."

"Bertha Lester. Yes, I *do* remember her. That tall queenly girl, who spent two summers in our village with her aunt, and was your 'dearest friend' while in your teens. Oh yes, I can almost see her now with her glossy black hair and lustrous eyes, her magnificent figure and step, and the splendid poise of her head, that set so many of our village beaux into ecstasies of admiration."

"Take care," laughed Annie, "or I shall be jealous of your glowing descriptions of her beauty. But she *was* a splendid looking girl, as we used to say at school. And then she had such aristocratic ideas: she was a perfect queen among the girls, and I thought it so appropriate a match when she married that wealthy young merchant, for her tastes and ambitions were far above the sphere her friends occupied. I have often wondered what had become of her—it is five years since her marriage—but I always thought of her as the star of some proud circle. And to think of her having lived for two years past upon a farm in the far West!"

"I should think her a poor subject for a farmer's wife," said Walter.

"Oh, it is too sad," said Annie mournfully. "She must be perfectly miserable. Such quiet, simple bodies as I am now, can be happy anywhere, but Bertha, with all her pride, beauty and refinement— her queenly manners, immured in a log hut in the wilderness! I am so sorry for her."

"Well Annie, how would you like to visit your old friend in her new home?"

"Are you in earnest, Walter?"

"Certainly, dearest. We have never spent any time in recreation since coming here. If you wish to go, I will hire a horse and carriage, and we will spend three days in visiting the Newcomes."

"Oh, I shall be delighted. Still, it will be a dreadful mortification to Bertha to see any one who knew her at home. But I will make her feel that she must not mind me, and perhaps be some comfort to her. How soon shall we go?"

"On Wednesday, if you can be ready."

"Oh yes, Freddy and I are soon made ready. What a delightful ride we will have in this lovely spring weather through the woods and plains of this wild, beautiful West."

It *was* a delightful ride, and enjoyed with a keen relish by the little party as they rode gaily along in the warm spring air, with new springing grass and bursting buds and flowers on every side. True, the roads were bad—*very* bad it must be acknowledged, being a mixture of the sort styled "corduroy" and the native mud and underbrush. But our young friends thought little of this, and laughed merrily over the joltings and discomforts of the journey. They had started at ten in the morning, and at nearly four in the afternoon came to a large double log house, with a sign before the door intimating that "entertainment" could be afforded to travelers therein.

"How far are we from Westville?" inquired Walter, as a tall, unmistakably *Yankee* figure appeared in the doorway.

"Well, we calculate it lies right about here," was the reply.

"But is there no village of that name?"

"Well, yes. I call this a village, that is it will be soon. The Post Office is here, and I keep tavern, and we expect a smart lot of folks in here to settle soon. Walk in sir, and I'll show you a map of the village— it's laid out grand."

Walter declined the invitation and enquired for the residence of Mr. Arthur Newcome.

"Mr. Newcome. Well, he lives about a mile on from here—straight on this road."

So our travelers moved on; and soon a neat log cabin, situated in a small natural grove and surrounded by flowering shrubs and vines, loomed up from a fine expanse of cleared land. A beautiful, dark-eyed boy of about four years, was playing before the door and watching him, and reading a

newspaper sat a sun browned but noble looking man
of about thirty years. He rose as Walter stopped his
horse at the foot of the path, outside the little gate,
and coming forward invited the travellers to alight
and enter the house. They complied, without making
themselves known, as Annie was anxious to see if
her early friend would recognize her. He led them
into a little room, fragrant with Spring blossoms and
green bushes, with a neat, homemade carpet on the
floor, plain but pretty furniture, and a large
melodeon in rosewood case, occupying a conspicuous place. Many a little article of tasteful workmanship graced the table and walls, and Annie, as
she looked about the little parlor bower, felt her pity
for her friend Bertha rapidly disappearing. And
when that lady herself appeared, with just the slight-
est matronly and dignified air added to her youthful charms, and recognized Annie almost at first
glance, welcoming her with the warmest expressions
of delight, the fears of the visitor as to her mortification at meeting early friends were entirely dis-
pelled. Still, Annie was puzzled and curious—
delighted, yet surprised, to find Bertha apparently
joyous and contented, where she had expected
despondency and repinings. The visit of condolence

and sympathy was turned to a mutual joyous meeting in a happy home. Her "queen" was actually washing dishes and scrubbing floors in the wilderness, and still happy and radiant with health and beauty. Surprise kept Annie almost silent, after their host had greeted them with frank, earnest welcomes, and the little ones on both sides had been duly admired—for in a little crib in the adjoining room lay a pair of twin cherubs, one year olds, sweet rose-buds with glowing cheeks, deep violet eyes, and rich clusters of brown curls, waiting to be seen and praised, with the boy brother and the stranger babe. And then came the tea—the nice preserved berries, the fresh bread and sweet butter, plain cake and dried venison, forming a meal to tempt the most fastidious appetite; and all prepared by the hands of Bertha herself. But after the meal, when the gentlemen had walked out to view the fields, and the dishes were swiftly washed and put away by both Bertha and Annie, and the babes sleeping, then the school-girl friends renewed their intimacy.

"And so you are surprised," said Bertha, "that I am happy here. Well, so I am at times, but oftener surprised that I could ever have sought for happiness elsewhere. I tell you Annie, I never enjoyed

such pure happiness as since we came to this pretty
forest home. You know that Arthur was rich when
we were married, and you know too that I used to
consider wealth and refinement and what is called
aristocracy,—though I could never clearly define the
word, can you?—as the only things worth living for.
We went immediately to Providence where Arthur
was a partner in a firm supposed to be the wealthi-
est in the city. And for nearly two years we lived in
the extreme of fashion and luxury. Our elegant residence was thronged by fashionable exquisites and
glittering, proud aristocrats. I was,—I may say it
now to you—the star of the magic circles I had so
longed to enter. But the bubble burst, and I saw all
that had been the aim of my life fading and receding
from my grasp. The sunshine in which I had basked
had proved but a meteor's glare. How I shuddered as
I looked to our future. The world seemed such a
wilderness. But then Annie, I found a new strength
in my being, and rose from the ruins of my false life
to live anew. With a few hundreds remaining from
our former wealth, we came here and made for ourselves this rustic home. We are healthful and happy.
And two months since, an old friend of my aunt's,
who had heard of our misfortunes, was so kind as to

send me this melodeon and a box of books, which in addition to those we had saved, make us a good library. And the benefit to my husband has been as great as to me. He has become a noble man in heart, soul and intellect full of strength, truth, courage and integrity. And oh, Annie, we have both become earnest sincere christians, which is best of all!"

The next day was spent by Walter and Annie with their friends, happily of course, and Friday afternoon saw them again traveling over the bad roads between Westville and Newburg.

"I have learned a lesson," said Annie. "One can be a queen in the forest as well as in the halls of society."

"Queen or not," said Walter, "she is her husband's 'crown' according to the Bible."

CHAPTER VIII

Perhaps there is no one thing in which we are so likely to err in the up building of society in this new land, as in too great adoration of what we term the *useful*. The money-seeking, speculative character of the dreams of many, lead them to denounce all that is elegant and beautiful simply, and many of the refining, softening influences of loveliness, are discarded, because they are not "useful." How this can be the case where the very air is filled with luxurious idleness, is a wonder; yet some there seem to be, who would almost chide the soft, sun-colored, lazy clouds in the summer skies, or look reprovingly upon the idle, fragrant flowers around our pathway; who would frown as the dallying, playful zephyrs kissed their cheeks; or the indolent, tuneful songsters of the wood raised their notes.

Yet we are ready to admit that *usefulness*—properly defined—is the great object of life—the only real beauty and grandeur. But what can be more repulsive than the many theories which would confine us solely to that which produces present, temporal and physical good? If to be useful one must eschew everything indolently lovely, or prettily graceful, and adhere only to the dull monotony of bread and butter life, then, dear reader, set us down as one determined to ignore *usefulness* forever, and cling to the unuseful things of earth. But we do not thus believe. And we have a favorite theory that much more of the happiness of life, especially in the domestic circle, lies in the exercise of some of the pretty, "unuseful" arts, than in all the precision, skill and industry of the most notable housewife. And so too, believed Annie Judson. Not that her house was not well and tidily kept—she regarded too much the comfort and punctuality of her husband to neglect that—but she believed domestic happiness to consist in something more than orderly, well cooked meals, faultless bosoms, and quiet children, however much these enter into the composition of bodily repose and comfort after labor. So she read recipes from her heart as well as her cook book, and considered kind words, smiles and gentle acts of love, *useful* when they brightened the eye and cheek of those she loved with answering smiles. And perhaps the unstudied polish, the courteous manners, the refinement of expressions and delicacy of taste of Walter Judson, was owing somewhat to the purity and choiceness of her words and sentiments, the careful attire, the glossy ringlets, the graceful elegance of her tastes—to the flowers blossoming in her window, the bird warbling in her room. Who can tell? At least, theirs was a very happy home, and Annie was its presiding genius. And so that little family circle lived on for two swift flying years when we will again look in upon them.

Three years have passed since they left the east. A pleasant little cottage home is theirs, with its small, but cheerful apartments, neat, white-fenced yard and garden, and growing shrubbery and fruit trees. Very slowly, to some of his scheming neighbors, but surely has Walter been surrounding himself with things which he may call his own. All had been gained by daily, manual labor, but in a place where labor commanded the compensation due to those who constitute the nobility of America's sons.

We will not attempt to portray the changes wrought in Newburg by those two years, or relate how it had grown from a promising village to the thriving, populous young city. And spring came again. Life swelled in the flower-buds, and breathed in the breezes. The leaflets danced and trembled till each seemed to contain a living soul full of hope and fear. The bright waters sparkled and gleamed in the sunlight, and anon laughed in rippling melody. All the works of man—the steam mills, the factories and warehouses—could not mar or destroy the beauty of those hills that guarded Newburg, or those vallies surrounding it. Nature here had resolved to thwart all such designs. She gave place for the flourishing business establishments but raised her monuments all around in defiance of monopoly. "Thus far shalt thou go and no farther" was written by her pen upon the rocky bluffs with their oaken coverings, and long will it be ere the warning shall be disregarded.

"I received a letter to-night from Henry Waters," said Walter as he left the tea-table, and drew a chair to the window which the vines were beginning to curtain with emerald leafiness.

"Ah, what does he write?" asked Annie.

"Inquires about the west, chiefly. He thinks of coming westward this spring, and wishes me to write to him of prospects here for his business. Now there is an excellent opening here for a good workman at the tinner's trade. I heard Wolcott saying yesterday that he would give high wages to one—and I believe Henry is master of his trade. But I fear he is not made of the right material for emigration here. He is too sanguine at first, too easily discouraged when the trial comes."

"I have always thought that if he had remained in the situation he was first placed in by his father after finishing his trade, he would have done well," remarked Annie.

"Yes, his father set him up well there; but he fancied he could do better, got discontented, sold everything at a sacrifice, and moved to another place. And I think he has several times destroyed equally good prospects by his impatience and discontent."

"Therefore you do not like to advise his removal west."

"No. It involves too much to be lightly decided upon. And I know so well the exaggerated ideas he will entertain, and the high hopes he will cherish, that I fear he will not be content with usual good success."

"Still I think you had better write him just what the prospects are, using no words calculated to inflame his fancy, and if he could come here without such exaggerated expectations he might do well."

"Which I had thought of doing. Henry is a fine, noble hearted fellow, and might do something in the world, if he would only give himself time." Walter sat down at a small, plain writing desk, produced paper, pens and ink from their places within it, and soon the letter was ready for its journey eastward. It needed no coloring from Walter's pen to warm the thoughts and raise the hopes of Henry Waters as he received it. Encouragement was enough, it mattered not how it was worded—his fertile fancy and glowing imagination filled up the picture in flattering colors, and bright air-castles loomed before his eyes, to become realities when he should reach the goal of his hopes, the West. Preparations were swiftly made, and the first of May saw himself, wife and two children the guests of the Judsons until a house could be rented, furniture procured, and themselves once more settled.

"This is the fifth time since our marriage that we have broken up and removed," said his wife to Annie. "Heaven grant it may be the last."

CHAPTER IX

The "new comers" were soon housekeeping by themselves, and Mr. Waters duly installed as foreman in the flourishing hardware establishment of Mr. Wolcott. The summer opened with much promise to Walter, as he had just closed a contract for building a large flouring mill under peculiarly advantageous circumstances. One thing only seemed adverse—as the warm weather came on both Annie and little Frederick seemed failing in health, and the fear of ague and fever, the dread of Western settlers ever, came to them with fresh terrors. These fears were reduced to certainty when, on entering the house at the dinner hour one warm day in July, Walter found his wife unable to rise, and shaking with the dreaded ague. But few days elapsed ere Fred too was alternately shivering and burning with the same disease. Then came unavailing searches for "help"; trials of young girls of all nations and tongues, from the most verdant Hibernian to the most uncouth Norwegian. But at last a kind, pleasant and capable Irish girl was found, order restored to the house so long a chaos under Walter's housekeeping, and the invalids, under the care and skill of a good physician, were fast recovering. The "chills" were broken up—but strengthening bitters were needed to drive the pallor from their cheeks, and restore the height of health to their eyes.

"And more than all else," said the doctor as he paid his last visit, "remember that you need to live regularly and quietly. You, Mrs. Judson, have not done this through the past spring. Your family was increased and your cares more than doubled by your friends' stay with you; the fatigue and anxiety predisposed you to the attack you have suffered. Do not overtask either body or mind, keep regular hours, and cheerful contented hearts, and your chances of escape from ague are twice those of the fearful, discontented, peevish person, who is constantly fancying he feels its approach."

August and September passed rapidly away—the health of his wife and child recovered. Walter had worked diligently and faithfully for the completion of his contracted work, employing several workmen in order to finish it in the required time. All was going on busily and prosperously, the home was now entirely their own, and the future seemed to promise all they hoped of comfort, improvement and happiness. But their friends and neighbors, the Waters family, began to show signs of uneasiness.

"I hardly think this is the place for me," said Henry to Walter one moonlight evening as they with their wives sat in the pretty parlor of the Judson's house. "I had hoped in coming West to free myself from the confinement and monotony of laboring for a stated price. It must be there are places in this region where I can by some bold stroke of tact or lucky turn of fortune, become independent of such toil."

"I don't know," said Walter. "I have worked hard since I came here, and expected to do so, but it may be that there are such chances as you speak of, though I hardly think that I should be willing to give up the *certainties* we have here in search of them."

"To what certainties do you refer?"

"To the almost absolute certainty of full compensation for our labor, and to the certainty that with that compensation we can make for ourselves *homes*. Our work commands a full reward here, which is seldom withheld; we can live cheaply, for the bounty of nature gives our farmers the means of providing our food at the lowest rates, and our surplus funds can be turned to the accumulation of property in these growing towns and villages, which is constantly increasing in value. So long as God gives me health to labor, and rewards that labor, so long I am content to toil for my livelihood."

"But do not think, Walter, that I am not equally willing to work. I think I cannot be called lazy, certainly; but now I have come so far to better my condition, I would like to be making money a little faster than in working by the day. And I believe—as I have nothing in particular to keep me here—that I shall go to Kansas or Nebraska this fall." And, unpersuaded by the experience and argument of Walter, the family were soon upon their way to a town in the extreme western section of Iowa, which Henry had concluded might be a profitable point for the realization of some of his cherished but undefined schemes.

Walter's job was nearly completed, and the money was already in the hands of the agent, to be paid to him at the closing of the given time, the first of November.

But on the night of the twentieth of October the cry of "fire" was heard, breaking the stillness. Hurrying footsteps went swiftly by, and the rattle of the engine—a new acquisition at Newburg—roused Walter from sleep just in time to hear the voice of one of his workmen at the gate, "Mr. Judson, the new mill is burning!" It was too true, and the work of months was swept away in an hour. No exertions could save the flaming building, and before morning nothing remained of it but a heap of smoking ruins. It was not till then the thought came into Walter's mind of the magnitude of his loss. The building was not yet delivered to the company for whom it was built. Not only the loss of his own time through that long summer and autumn, but the wages of those whom he had hired to assist him, were involved. He hastened home to consult and sympathize with his wife in this new and fearful trial.

"There is no other way, Walter," she said, almost calmly, after they had spoken of the sad catastrophe for some time, "we must give up our home. Accept the offer you had one month ago, and sell this place, and the price will enable you to pay your men. They are poor, have but just arrived here, and may suffer for want before you can accumulate it in other ways."

"But what shall we do?" asked Walter. "All I have will but pay these debts—scarcely that, and the winter is almost here. I have no work on hand of any importance, and when our house is gone we are worse off than ever before."

"I know it, but it is theirs, not ours. They must be paid if possible. You are better known here, and can do many things which they cannot. Miles has seven children and as yet no comfortable place to shelter them. Bradley's family are sick and depending upon this money for comforts during the winter."

"You are right, Annie; it shall be done. We will trust in the One who has said: 'I will never leave thee nor forsake thee.'"

After a pause:

"How I wish I had now the money I laid out in land. I fear that was a foolish investment.—It may be that I can sell it. I must try; but I fear it cannot be done in time to furnish these men the means of subsistence." And Walter's voice grew husky, for this loss to him was just as great as *yours* was, Sir Millionaire, when the house of which you were a partner broke, and hundreds of thousands went down in the ruin. You have retrieved your fortunes—so may he—but there was no sincere grief in your heart at leaving that princely house in Fifth Avenue, than now swelled in his at leaving the humble home he had so long and faithfully toiled for.

But it was given up. The sacrifice had been resolved upon—it was necessary, and the sooner it was accomplished the better for the feelings of that little home circle. Even little Fred, now a fine, sturdy boy of four years, brushed back his tears at parting with his pet flowers, and his own little garden, and, following Mamma's example, would not cry before Papa. The sale was accomplished, and the next week must witness their removal from the pleasant cottage home.

It was their intention to rent again the house in which they had first lived, and Walter had some work engaged, and a hope of procuring sufficient to support them during the winter. What course he should take when spring came, he had not yet decided. Perhaps he could sell the land—perhaps he should find it best to commence again the accumulation of funds sufficient to purchase another lot, and build again in this place—perhaps it might be best to remove from Newburg to some newer settlement, where the home they were still resolved upon might be purchased more cheaply.

Once more settled in the house which had been the scene of their early efforts, Walter and Annie strove again to look hopefully to the future, when, on going to the post office one day, he received a letter which was the herald of his future success in a new field of effort.

CHAPTER X

The letter mentioned in the preceding chapter, was from a settler in the neighborhood in which lay Walter's purchase of land, stating that the township was becoming thickly settled and land much more valuable than formerly: that at about the point occupied by his land, it was thought best to establish a store, mills, &c., for the accommodation of the surrounding farmers, and requesting Mr. Judson to visit the locality and decide what could be done in the matter. Business men, who knew better than he the spirit of enterprise and speculation, advised him to attend at once to what might be a most advantageous opportunity of disposing of his property, and Walter resolved to go, though at first he could scarcely credit the statement that the wilds in which he had located his claim, had become a populated farming region. The journey was not now made as before on horseback, for stages had daily established routes to connect the interior of the State with its eastern towns and cities, and through them with the great world beyond. Each day revealed to him the changes wrought in the short time since he travelled the same route before. The almost boundless prairies, where he rode for many miles without seeing a human form, now presented the appearance of an old and long cultivated country. Comfortable farm houses stood upon the rolling mounds, over-looking the smooth, neatly fenced fields, and surrounded by clumps of beautiful trees of natural growth, while near by, the thrifty nursery and young orchard gave promise of future fruitfulness. Here and there a church spire pointed upward, and a school house play ground with its merry troop met his eye. The wealth of the soil and beauty of the country were evident, and it was also clearly to be seen that those who came there with scarcely funds sufficient to buy these broad acres at the lowest rates, were amassing fortunes from the abundant yielding of their hidden stores. And Walter knew as he gazed upon these plain, substantial dwellings, that they sheltered many a family, whose home had previously been in the dark, noisome, crowded street of some teeming city, many a one escaped from the thralldom of mine, factory and workshop to a more congenial life. Here the oppressed of every land were finding rest and prosperity. Colonies from almost every European country were settled or settling upon the wide expanse of rich, beautiful prairie lands.—German, Irish, Norwegian, Welsh, French, and Swede were represented in the newly formed communities, yet ever mixed with the ever-present, persevering Yankee. Ah, *they* have found "a home in the West" to be no fiction, and thank God that this world which He has made holds room for all His children. And removed from the scenes of vice with which city life is so prolific, many a soul which had been led into the paths of sin, throws off the shackles of immorality, and lives a new life amid the pure freshness of nature.

Walter was partially prepared for the changes in the place of his destination by those he had noticed upon the way. After consultation with some of the most substantial and reliable of the neighboring farmers, it was decided to lay out a part of his land into town lots, to sell immediately to men then present, locations for a store, mill and cabinet shop. To induce mechanics, merchants and professional men to become residents in as great numbers as possible; in fact, to establish "a paper city,"—and Walter its proprietor!

"And let me hope, Mr. Judson, that you will make my house your home while attending to your business here," said a fine, intelligent looking man of about forty–five years, whose farm lay adjoining Walter's domain, which was suddenly becoming of so much importance. The invitation was thankfully accepted, and he found himself domesticated with an agreeable, interesting family, consisting of his host, Mr. Leonard, his wife, a pleasing, motherly lady of forty, his eldest son, who had just reached twenty–one, and was studying for medical practice, in Cincinnati, but was now visiting his parents, and two lovely young sisters of sixteen and fourteen years. Their manners and conversation indicated refinement and intelligence, and though living as yet in a log house of ample dimensions, and following the vocations of a farmer's life, there was grace and polish in all their surroundings that spoke of the highest respectability in their former associations. Indeed, during the second day Walter learned that Mr. Leonard had been a lawyer in large practice in an eastern city, but longing for a country life, had closed his business, gathered his savings and emigrated hither. "My wife and the girls were crazed to come to the West—did not like city life—wife was brought up on a farm and kept the girls by turns at their grand-parents, learning to make butter and cheese. I was tired of meddling with other people's quarrels—so here we are. We have been here a year and a half—like it well—are healthy and happy; and if your new town don't drive us farther back, here we shall stay the balance of our lives. How is it, wife, shall we sell out and leave to get away from civilization again?" "Wife" looked as if she thought it hardly necessary just at present, and the lively imaginations of the girls were already at work speculating upon the growth of the new village.

Arrangements went forward rapidly—streets and building lots were laid out on the smooth green meadows, and a site for a mill was purchased by a gentleman already there, at whose instance Walter had been summoned,—another lot for a store was sold to a young man, son of one of the settlers, who thus expended his small savings during a five years' clerkship,—and the embryo town received the name of Hastings, from Walter, in compliment to the parents of his wife.

When he returned to Newburg at the end of two weeks, he had received two hundred dollars in cash from the sale of these lots, and seen preparations made for immediate erection of the buildings. Winter would retard the work somewhat, but with the opening of Spring they hoped to progress rapidly. Two or three mechanics had already removed there from a neighboring county, hiring rooms and board of the adjacent farmers, while working upon them. Had it not been for the near approach of cold weather, and the long journey by stage, Walter would have resolved upon a removal thither himself, but thought it best deferred till Spring. So with a new phase of Western enterprise before him, and new hopes in his heart, he returned to his family and labor for the winter.

Annie's playful rallying of Walter's "speculations" was mixed with the deepest thankfulness. "We have done right," she would say, "in giving up our little home here to supply the necessities of those poor men, and Providence has rewarded us by giving us another, and so ordering it that we can reside there in comfort and prosperity, while we thought of it only as a wilderness."

So in resignation to His will, without whom not a
sparrow falls to the ground, and in bright hopes for
the future, passed another winter, and ere its close,
a cradled babe slept while rocked by Fred, who was
loud in the praises of his sister Dora. Annie had
given it her mother's name, Theodora,—the gift of
God.

We must not forget the young French wife of
Gerald Lefay, whose sweet face so interested Annie
during her first summer's residence in Iowa. She
was supplied with work liberally by the ladies of
Newburg, who became acquainted with her story
through Annie, and she continued to reside in her
little upper room, patiently waiting and hoping. She
was enabled by her earnings to procure comfortable
furniture and clothing for the winter, and not many
babes in Newburg were there, which were not robed
in her delicately embroidered dresses, shoes, and
sacques. As time passed, she gained friends, and her
gentle manner, and girlish face, with her sad experience, made all who knew her vie in kindness to the
lonely, bereaved girl-wife.—And as time passed, her
pensive beauty and delicate accomplishments won
the heart of an honest, intelligent young shoemak-
er with a pretty rural home of his own just outside

the Newburg city limits, and in the third year of her residence there, she was urged to become his wife. No one could believe her husband was living—he had doubtless fallen a prey to some fatal disease before her arrival. But she could not give up the hope of meeting him again. And at length, when by the advice of friends, she sent to France for proofs of her marriage, and they arrived accompanied by urgent entreaties for her return, steps were taken to secure the property her husband had bought, now become valuable to her. But she could not go home— here was the last trace of him she loved, and here she would remain until all hope was destroyed by certainty.

And well was such constance rewarded, for during the winter we have mentioned, as the last spent by the Judsons in Newburg, there came by the stage one night, a noble looking stranger, who, scarcely alighted, inquired for Celeste Lefay. Known to many, as she was, he was directed to her residence. We will not desecrate that interview by words, but only relate the causes of their long separation. The vessel in which Celeste came to New York had been several days behind her usual time on the trip, and on his arrival there to meet her, there was a rumor of the

loss of the ship and all on board. Not waiting to
ascertain its truth, the young husband hastened to
New Orleans, and thence to Cuba, thinking that his
friends might have taken other vessels than they
first designed and bound for these ports. When this
hope was gone, he regarded her loss as certain, and
fatigue and anxiety brought on a severe illness from
which it was months ere he recovered. A sea voyage
being recommended, he embarked for France, but
before reaching there, dreading to meet the parents
of Celeste and inform them of her loss, he exchanged
ships and sailed for South America. After spending
two years there, he again resolved to visit his early
home, and arrived in France soon after the replies to
her letters requesting proofs of her marriage were
sent. "Thinking I would be the strongest proof," he
said with a true French levity, yet with earnest devotion in his looks and manner, "I hastened after them.
If I had only gone to France when I first started, how
fortunate for us, for I found they knew of your residence and welfare constantly. But you are restored
to me at last, my bride, my sweet Celeste, and we
shall be happy. Here is where I designed making our
home, but when I lost you I could not bear to return
to my purchase and the scenes I had hoped to enjoy

in your society. I spent one month here just before going to New York, and selected the land which was bought for me by an old French gentleman here, since dead, while I was on my way."

"Yes," said Celeste, "he died just before my arrival here,—but let these years of darkness be forgotten. Tell me of my home, my parents, sisters and brothers, tell me of yourself and of our future, and let us be glad and thankful that the light has dawned at last."

CHAPTER XI

Early in April Walter was prepared for a removal to the new village. The journey was not a pleasant one, for the roads were yet very much unsettled and the Spring rains had made them extremely muddy, yet they arrived with sound though weary limbs on the fourth day after leaving Newburg. Mr. Judson found the large flouring mills nearly completed, and a commodious store in process of erection, and received offers immediately for several building lots. —We will not particularize the progress of the growth of "Hastings" during the spring and summer. It received however a fair share of the emigration then settling into the beautiful valley in which it was situated, and a good and healthy patronage from the fine farming region around. Walter found himself suddenly becoming of more consequence than he had anticipated a few months previously, yet was somewhat startled at seeing himself spoken of as the "wealthy and energetic proprietor of the beautiful and thriving town of Hastings," in the paper located in an adjoining county. But he bore his honors "blushingly" as became a modest man, and labored "working with his own hands" at his trade during the entire summer. And when Autumn came, they had once more a home. A house had been erected, which was really beautiful and commodious. Trees and shrubbery were procured and set, a yard and garden fenced, and all was ready for the occupants who had spent the summer with the pleasant family of Mr. Leonard while waiting for the erection of their residence. And Walter was enabled from the sale of lots to pay for all his own improvements and maintain his little family in comfort. And in the golden October days, the little community numbered some twenty families, most of whom had, or were building small but neat dwellings and shops. And just before the winter a fresh arrival, consisting of a young lawyer and his bride, an elderly minister with his three motherless children, and a young niece as teacher of a school through the winter, was duly announced by the delighted ladies of Hastings to each other. A lot had been given, a subscription raised, and a small church was already being erected, which would serve as school-room until the school-house could be built the ensuing summer. And so winter came for the first time upon the little village, and its inhabitants, and shut them from the busy world without their narrow limits; but with contented, hopeful hearts, and a sufficiency of all physical comforts, they contrived to make those months pass most pleasantly and swiftly. And as they could number eight young gentlemen of usual intelligence and agreeability, and five or six young ladies from the ages of sixteen to twenty five, two of whom possessed and played pianos, besides several couple of newly married people, we must not imagine that hope had all to do with the pleasures of that winter. A great deal of real social enjoyment could be and was extracted from the occasional meetings of these sojourners in the "wilderness." It is true they knew little of the most interesting or latest topic of gossip among the "elite" of the distant cities, and still less of the fashions in dress which occupy so much of the time of the "beau monde." But the former could well be spared, while they talked of first impressions of the West, hopes for the future, and discussed ideas and plans for improvements in all about them. Even young ladies of the fashionable "butterfly stamp" learned to feel an intense interest in mill-dams, saw-logs, rafts and railroads, when they considered how intimately these were connected with the parlors, side walks, and elegant furniture they longed for. And as to fashions, those latest from the East lent patterns and described costumes to the more unsophisticated, while the fashion plates of the few magazines taken in town, were duly studied by all. At any rate, in the opinion of the gentlemen, the young ladies of Hastings dressed very prettily and economically too, and were very much to be admired; and their eyes grew brighter and their cheeks rosier as they quaffed the nectar of health from the pure frosty air of the northwestern winter. We doubt if any fashionable belle in the circles of upper-ten-dom passed that winter more joyously, or came out of it with such bloom and spirits as these western maidens. And as a matter of course, Master Cupid was there too—the everywhere-present elf—and when Spring came there were two or three pairs of loving hearts which had discovered strange sympathies with each other, and some manly lips, which uttered the trifling compliments and fashionable common-places of half a dozen winters in "society" with indifference, whispered tender words with a manner strangely at variance with their usual studied unconcern.—And then there were weddings, one in the little church—and two others soon after at home with all the village for guests, in the new and yet unfurnished parlors; and the brides wore plain white muslins with natural wild flowers in their soft hair, in lieu of the unobtainable orange blossoms and white rose buds, and looked as pretty and bride like as if robed in the costliest "moise" and richest Brussels or Mechlin. It does not take much after all to teach us how little of real happiness depends upon what we used to consider almost the indispensables of existence; one years' residence where all real and few fancied wants are supplied, will fill the heart with new thoughts of life and its duties, and away from all the pomp and glitter of folly's votaries, higher resolves and nobler purposes assert supremacy, and few are the hearts so utterly given up to frivolity, that they do not thrill to the touch of the new-inspired, life ennobling sentiments.

"Ah," says some fair reader, "but if the rapidity of your progress be continued, you must soon have milliners and tailors, with all their laces, ribbons, silks, and broadcloths, and in daily receipt of the latest French fashions, settled among you. Then we shall see the effects of your new life and exalted sentiments."

My dear lady, we shall be very glad to welcome them. But we cannot believe that the feelings of which we have spoken, and which are veritable realities to so many who have left "the world" and gone to begin a little one of their own, which in time may become a part of the greater, can make their home in any heart, even for a short time, without leaving traces of their residence there. And though we shall not object to the wearing of so many of the beautiful and fashionable things they bring us, as our own taste and the pockets of fathers and husbands will allow, still there will be a trace of the angel's visit,— the angel that presides over quiet, domestic scenes, and pure, heartfelt, contented happiness, and we shall never be again, if we ever have been, the thoughtless votaries of fashion and the giddy followers of display and notoriety. Life has appeared to us in her nobler characters, and no mask can make us forget her improved features. But we must beg pardon for this long digression—for really it was very awkward in us to leave those fair young brides just at the most interesting moment, that of the marriage ceremony, and go off into this homily upon fashion, and the lessons the woods and prairies have taught us. Still, you know all that we could tell you of these joyous occasions, is just how happy they all were, and just how every one laughed at what each one said, though the same things had been said at every wedding since Adam's. A wedding is one of the things of which we never tire—it is always "new and interesting." And we will only tell you that the prettiest of the pretty cottages built in Hastings that spring and summer, were designed for the occupancy of those fair ladies who had cast their lot irrevocably with the pioneers of refinement and civilization in the far West.

CHAPTER XII

Dr. Leonard's studies were finished, the long coveted diploma received, and with all his new professional dignity, and arrived at the mature age of twenty-three, he was visiting again at his parents' home. With all his knowledge of Western growth and improvement, he could scarcely believe his own senses on viewing the changes since he last left his father's roof;—the neat white houses, and quiet, though thrifty air of the little town were very pleasing too, to the study wearied young man. And though he had come home only for a visit previous to selecting a situation for a permanent location in the practice of his profession, not many days had elapsed before he began to consider seriously the question of a settlement *here*, and to see in imagination the sign of "Hervey Leonard, M.D." gracing a conspicuous situation on the main street of Hastings. And so it came to pass that considerations and fancies

assumed more and more the shape of realities until
Mr. Leonard, Sr., having been consulted and advised
with, an office was actually being built, the sign
aforesaid ordered, and after a long meditated trip
eastward, and the purchase of the necessary library,
Dr. Leonard would become the resident physician of
Hastings. Hervey Leonard, being the first young
gentleman formally introduced to our readers,
deserves to be described in all the glowing terms
romance allows in speaking of her heroes. Truth,
however, compels us to allow that very many of those
personal charms so admired by sentimental young
ladies, were not granted to him by Nature, she probably not being aware that we should ever stand in
need of him as a hero. So we shall be obliged to take
him as he was, with hair of very common brown,
instead of "black, curling locks," and eyes of clear,
kindly blue, in place of the "dark, proud speaking
orbs" so necessary to the proper appearance of the
hero aforesaid. Then his form was neither tall nor
very graceful, but of medium height, and fully the
usual amount of awkwardness and embarrassment
so troublesome to young men who have spent more
time in study than in society. We must own that his
mother and sisters would not agree with all our

description, for in their eyes Hervey was *handsome* and his manners the most pleasing and agreeable— but partial mothers and sisters cannot be allowed to establish the criterion of manly beauty and attraction—were this permitted we fear many a graceful, splendid looking Adonis would have to resign his station, and many a plain, awkward but kind and attentive son and brother, would be promoted. We believe Hervey was content with the praises and love of his affectionate admirers at home, and thought little more about the matter.

After a few weeks at home, the eastern journey to their former home was taken, and he, having made the acquaintance of Walter and Annie Judson, and become the favorite playfellow of Fred, and received the baby smiles and admiration of Dora, was commissioned to bear to the old Connecticut home many a message of love and remembrance; for a visit to the home of Annie's parents would take him but thirty miles from his course, and she well knew the pleasure such a visit would confer. The sight of one known and prized by our friends is next to seeing themselves. So letters of introduction were written, and with many good wishes and bright hopes the journey was commenced.

It is very strange, but we must tell the truth, that that visit which in prospect was to last but three weeks, was lengthened into ten. And we must give Hervey credit for the most earnest desire to fulfill the wishes of Annie and deliver all her messages, when we find that three times during his stay in Hartford, he rode the entire distance to the residence of Mr. Hastings, spending three or four days with the family at each.—But doubtless those two last visits were caused by the remembrance of some neglected errand from the Judsons. It could not be that Mary Hastings, now a beautiful girl in her twentieth summer, had anything to do with them, or that the young physician's heart was taken captive by her smiles and gentle performance of the home-duties. Yet it must be acknowledged that during his last visit there, there was a pleasant moonlight walk taken, during which something unusually interesting must have been said, for on her return Mary was strangely absent-minded, and her pretty face covered with blushes.—And we have good reasons for believing that delicately enveloped letters passed often over the many miles between them after his return to Hastings. Yet these are things in which gossips deal, and we will drop the subject, lest we incur the bestowal of the name.

"A letter from Henry Waters, Annie!" said Walter, looking up from the examination of the evening mail.

"Is he still at Rockville?"

"No, he has been in two or three places since leaving there. Says he cannot find that the West is any more favorable a field of labor than the East: that he thinks he has had ample opportunities for judging as he has visited many places in Iowa, Kansas and Nebraska since leaving here."

"What does he propose doing?"

"Oh, he thinks he shall return to the East. His family too, have been sick,—no wonder, that—he has kept them in a continual fatigue and excitement— and he indulges in the most violent abuse of the whole western country, its people, climate, prospects and natural features, and says that once more settled at home, 'no persuasion of friends' will ever again lead him to forsake the eastern world."

"Which I most heartily hope will be the case," said Annie laughingly. "I pity his wife and children, and really Henry himself might become something worth while, if he would turn his attention to improvement in his station and advancement of his interests where he really is well located, instead of ever seeking to make good better by a change."

"He is too uneasy to do well anywhere, I fear," responded Walter, "but his present object in addressing me is to solicit the loan of twenty–five dollars, which I will send him, with the advice to use it in going East if he is determined upon it, and to stay when he gets there. He is not the stuff western men should be composed of."

"And give my love to poor Carrie and the children. How I wish they had the home, prospects and happiness we possess in the land they seem to find so unfortunate."

And Annie cast a fond look at her healthy, rosy-cheeked little ones in their pretty dresses, and then a proud, confiding smile upon her husband.

During the month of September, the second year of their residence in Hastings, Arthur Newcome and his wife made a visit to the Judsons. Bertha as beautiful and queenly as ever, though the mother of four lovely children, and as she laughingly asserted, "their school-ma'am too." For with a touch of the old pride, she preferred keeping her darlings at home, to sending them the long walk to the Westville schoolhouse with the children of the neighboring farmers.

The log house had been displaced and a pleasant cottage of tasteful appearance took its place; but Westville, from some fault in its location had not grown with the swiftness of other "paper towns," and they were still nearly destitute of refined and intellectual society.

"And are you never lonely?" said Annie. "Do you never long for the adoration and appreciation of society?"

"Society!" and she pointed to the little group playing near the door. "My heart is full.—With the care of those dear ones, my noble, princely boy, my twin rose-buds Ella and May, and this last precious gift, my baby Frank, I have no time for the claims of others. I read much, for we are well supplied with literature by the kindness of friends and our own subscriptions and purchases, and I find ample use for all I may learn in companionship and conversation with my husband, and the training of my children. And if I succeed in making them happy in the present and useful in the future, I shall feel that my mission is fulfilled nor ask for a higher or more brilliant sphere of action and influence."

CHAPTER XIII

The little community at Hastings continued to be prosperous and hopeful, while Walter Judson found himself rapidly accumulating wealth and influence in consequence. He had come westward with the expectations only of earning a comfortable livelihood by manual labor, and feeling that with that he could be content. Yet he now found himself beyond the necessity of that daily toil which had gained for him his first "home in the west," and surrounded by circumstances and associations beyond his most sanguine hopes. But to very few comes such full and unhoped success; and Walter felt that to him had been awarded more than to most of them who seek employment and homes in a new land.

Their new home was a most beautiful one—trees and shrubbery of rare varieties were beginning to adapt themselves to the new soil, while among them, carefully tended, bloomed many native flowers.

Vines, wreathed with verdure, pretty arches and arbors, and walks, were laid out and nicely finished through all the grounds. In the interior of the house, Annie's refined tastes and skilful fingers had accomplished wonders, situated, as they were, so far from the elegances of the fashionable upholstery and cabinet wares.

It was a truly lovely spot, and the sweet, still girlish face of Annie and the pure, artless beauty of their little ones, made it almost a paradise to the home loving Walter.

Winter came again, but ere its coming our friends are introduced to different scenes.

"How would you like to spend the winter at home, Annie?" asked Walter one late October evening.

"Are you really in earnest?"

"Surely, I am. And if you will promise not to betray me, I will let you into the secret of a little plot I have been getting up for the especial surprise of our fair sister Mary. Hervey came to me to-day and with sundry blushes and much embarrassment contrived to tell me that he expects to visit the east again this winter, and to become our brother on New Year's Eve. Of course I lectured him duly upon such extravagance in a young physician, to think of taking such a journey twice within a year, but he only replied by proposing that we should accompany him. I assured him that it would not be possible on account of some business which would require my especial care during that time, which I really thought was the case, but to night have received letters which place it in a different shape. And now we can go, I think, if you wish it, and by keeping Hervey in ignorance of the change in our plans, will give them quite a surprise if not some pleasure."

"How soon will he go?"

"By the first of December. We will follow by the next week, at farthest, and arrive in time to tease Mary sufficiently before the wedding." And Walter laughed heartily, and was evidently quite happy at the prospect.

Going home! Annie could hardly realize it, yet her heart was overflowing at the thought.—She had heard from Mary of her engagement, and looked forward with joy to the time when they should be re-united. She had even thought of a visit home, at the time of their wedding, as perhaps *possible*, but the almost certainty swelled her heart with thankfulness. Those weeks of preparation were busy ones to both hands and mind, and her anxious care to have Freddy and Dora appear to the best advantage to those far away loved ones, brought many an amused smile to Walter's beaming face.

"And how will that do, papa, to wear at aunt Mary's wedding?" she asked one night presenting children for his inspection. Fred was dressed in a bright purple velvet coat or sacque, with soft white merino pants and neatly fitting gaiters; Dora in pure soft folds of white merino, embroidered with lilac leaves and flowers:—the same colors were predominant in both.

"Beautiful," exclaimed "papa," looking admiringly at the pretty little ones. Annie was not quite sure which were meant—the children or the dresses.

"Do you know, Annie," he said musingly, as she proceeded to enrobe the little forms, and fold the white night robes about them, "do you know that there is some difference in the feelings with which we prepare for this journey, and those with which we made arrangements for the removal West?"

"Ah yes. Then our hearts were full of doubt and care. Our hopes, though strong, were vague, our plans very humble, our anguish at parting with friends, deep, and the future seemed so uncertain through the mist of those parting tears!"

"But it was 'all for the best,' dear Annie. Had we remained there, our lives and those of our children, would have been clouded with care and strife for daily bread which now *they* may never know."

"True, Walter. We certainly have never yet seen reason to regret it." And she looked complacently round the cosy sitting room with its really elegant furniture. "But I am so glad to go home!" she added, as her thoughts again wandered to that distant fireside, and the faces of those surrounding it.

The evening before Dr. Leonard's departure came, and a part of it, was spent with the Judsons. It needed all Fred's self command, together with many warning glances from his mother, to keep the little tongue from betraying the important secret. But it was kept, though had the visitor heeded the prattle of little Dora he might have guessed it. But the baby-talk was strangely unheeded, for his thoughts were wanderers in advance of his form that night, and he was picturing the welcome he should soon receive from a fair maiden some thousand miles away.

The intended journey was no secret as soon as Hervey was gone, and good Mr. Leonard and his family laughed heartily at the anticipated surprise.

An addition was made to the party too of the eldest sister of Hervey, Annie protesting that she could not do without her assistance in taking care of the children, and the young girl joyfully accepting the opportunity of being present at her only brother's wedding.

And on the third morning after Dr. Leonard's departure, the happy party were also upon the way eastward and homeward. A journey by stage and cars, has never been considered especially pleasing in winter, yet a view of the happy faces of that group would have led one to suppose that it was one of the most agreeable of recreations.

We shrink from the task of depicting the scene when the loaded sleigh stopped at the door of Mr. Hastings, and the well known form of Walter leaped from his seat, and hastily unloading the weary travelers, marched at their head up the little gravel walk to the front door. The surprise was complete, and the puzzled expression of Hervey's face as he regarded the unexpected group during their joyful welcome, was not lost to Walter's fun loving eye. And there were joyful exclamations and hurried shaking of hands and kisses,—the mother's voice murmured a blessing over the wondering children, while the father's burst forth in a prayer of thankfulness that he had lived to see this hour.

And when they all grew calmer with the dear assurance of their joy, how proudly every eye rested upon the noble, manly face of Walter, the *sweet* and gentle one of Annie, and the pure beauty of their children! Fred was almost certain that he remembered "uncle Edward" ere an hour had passed, and baby Dora was the pet and admiration of the household. The morning light came in at the windows before they had all left that old familiar hearth stone, for the united sisters could not rest with that wild tide of joy flowing from heart to heart.—So they sat and talked of the future alone, when the last ones, father and mother—had left them by the glowing grate. And if Annie was gladdened and surprised at the blooming beauty, and charming manners of her sister, Mary was not less so at the gentle dignity and matron grace of one so long immured in the "western wilds." And when morning came, the news had spread to other homes, and old friends crowded in to welcome the wanderers back. So there was gladness and true heart-music in that humble home for three swift flying weeks, and then came the wedding, which Mary laughingly declared to Annie she would be glad to have done with, just to silence Walter's teasing about it.

CHAPTER XIV

That sweet Addie Leonard must be her bridesmaid, was fully decided by Mary before the close of the first day after their arrival, and "brother Henry," the grave, thoughtful young lawyer, would stand beside Hervey in the trying moment. They were married by the same pastor who had united Walter and Annie, in the same church, and returned by the clear moonlight of the New Year's eve to partake of the feast of good things which had been provided by Mrs. Hastings and a pretty, dark-eyed cousin who came to spend the week with them.

Dr. Leonard's radiant face looked the very personification of happiness during the long merry evening, while Mary's blushes grew deeper as Walter gravely rallied her upon the extreme impropriety of her conduct in so hastily falling in love with a stranger.

"I shall hold you personally responsible for that," said Mr. Hastings "not content with taking Annie from us, you have plainly headed the conspiracy to rob us of our last daughter, under the pretext of making him the bearer of letters from you. I suppose you young folks in your happiness have never once thought of what mother and I will do when you are gone."

The faces of Annie and Mary showed that they *had* thought of it, while both Hervey and Walter's laughing eyes grew thoughtful. It would surly be a saddened home, when the parents in failing health and declining years should miss the soft step and gentle voice of their youngest daughter. The last parting threatened to be more trying than the first.

"Dear father," said Walter's deep, manly voice, "Why will you not *all* go with us? I think we can get up quarrels enough in our quiet neighborhood to keep Henry busy in settling them, if we cannot employ him more usefully still, and Edward is already longing for one of those beautiful farms I have described to him in our bright Iowa. Then you and mother can remain with us, or live by your-selves, as you choose."

"Thank you, thank you, Walter; but our home here—"

"Can easily be sold, I presume. I know it will be hard to leave it, but—"

"Not as hard as to stay by a deserted hearth-stone," interrupted Mr. Hastings. "You are right, Walter, there is nothing to keep my children here. Henry's legal studies are now finished, and he must go elsewhere for practice, for here the profession is full; Edward is wearing out life and patience in the drudgery of a clerkship, while his predilections are for a farmer's life, which he can never pursue here. We can't stay alone; can we, mother?"

"No, Frederick," answered the tremulous voice of "mother,"—tremulous with tears of joy and thankfulness; "let us go with them. If they have room and home for us there, and Henry and Edward will join them, we can gladly give up old associations and scenes for the sake of being with our children.— The best children in the world," she added with a proud glance through her tears.

Then followed general plans, remarks and suggestions from all sides. Henry, who had never before expressed a serious intention of going westward, now seconded the movement, while Edward, whose conviction of duty had kept him with his parents during all his longings for a rural life, was overjoyed at the proposed removal.

The glad faces of the sisters told how full of joy they were at the prospect of an unbroken family circle in their distant home. Hervey had been silent, but not uninterested, for he well knew that this decision would remove the only weight that depressed the buoyant spirits of his bride; while Addie was in ecstacies at the prospect of such an addition to the society at Hastings.

Not only that evening but several subsequent ones were the arrangements for their final reunion discussed and plans matured. And the remaining weeks of the winter passed swiftly amid their preparations, though the young people found time for a week amid the gayeties and sight seeing of New York.

Early in spring all was ready. The old homestead was sold to a rich neighbor, who designed it as the residence of his only son, just married to the dark-eyed cousin of the Hastings family, whom we met at Mary's wedding.

And the family party were on their journey— father and mother, Walter and Annie, with their children, the handsome, manly brothers, and the young physician with his bride,—speeding towards the little villages in far Iowa which bore their family name, where they arrived safely in due time.

But once more, ere we bid them farewell, will we join that family gathering.

A year has passed since their arrival. They are all sitting in the parlor of Dr. Leonard's just finished residence, where a prominent object of interest seems to be a sweet babe of two months in Mary's arms. And they are speaking of the past, the present and future, with cheerful hearts, for life is bright before each member of that group. "Edward's farm," as it was called, though purchased with the price of the homestead, will soon boast a house, and rumor says a mistress in the person of Miss Addie Leonard. Henry's office and sign are side by side with those of Hervey, while he is as yet an inmate of their home. Mrs. and Mrs. Hastings remain with Annie, and, though Edward talks of their removal to his new home on its completion, she gravely assures him that mother will never leave her, and the children cannot spare "grandpa"—he is too good a playfellow.

. . .

Walter Judson, the humble young mechanic, the patient toiler in the fields of manual and intellectual labor, has met a full reward. A reward which does not always crown earnest effort and faithful trust in Providence, yet one which is seldom sought thus. His early education improved with studious energy, has won for him standing and influence among the noblest where all have worked out their own nobility, and he has just returned from filling his seat in the legislature of his adopted and beloved State.

"Yes," he said in reply to a remark of Henry's, "we have been prospered here. 'The west,' has been to us a fond mother, and such she will prove to all who seek her for herself, and ask a home within her wide spread arms. She loves the honest, persevering laborer, and speeds his efforts to obtain what is so often denied to the humble toiler in older lands— a home. But for those who seek to escape from God's great ordinance of labor—labor of hand, heart or brain,—the only true nobility—her welcome is less cordial. She offers room and opportunity and full reward *for* toil—not immunity—from it. Hers is no fabulous treasure, no glittering mine, no golden promise of boundless wealth, but she proffers freedom to the wearied, ill paid sons of labor.

Freedom for the expansion of heart, soul and mind. Freedom to stretch the aching limbs and breathe in strength and energy from her winds. Freedom from the harassing necessities of scanty paid toil, and daily want of food. Her fair fields repay abundantly the labor bestowed upon them, and fill to over-flowing the store-houses of those who never before possessed a week's supply of provision in advance. And to the disheartened, burdened, and despond-ing, everywhere, she extends the invitation to come and partake freely of all she has to give—room for action and assurance of reward and appreciation. She wants no idlers—but earnest, ardent, zealous working men. And such shall gain 'A HOME IN THE WEST' not always as humble as the hopes and efforts which essay to obtain it."

Other Bur Oak Books of Interest

"All Will Yet Be Well"
The Diary of Sarah Gillespie
Huftalen, 1873–1952
By Suzanne L. Bunkers

The Folks
By Ruth Suckow

Letters of a German
American Farmer
Jürnjakob Swehn
Travels to America
By Johannes Gillhoff

My Vegetable Love
A Journal of a Growing Season
By Carl H. Klaus

Nothing to Do but Stay
My Pioneer Mother
By Carrie Young

Prairie Cooks
Glorified Rice, Three-Day Buns,
and Other Reminiscences
By Carrie Young with
Felicia Young

Prairie Reunion
By Barbara J. Scot

A Ruth Suckow Omnibus
By Ruth Suckow

"A Secret to Be Burried"
The Diary and Life of Emily
Hawley Gillespie, 1858–1888
By Judy Nolte Lensink

Sarah's Seasons
An Amish Diary and
Conversation
By Martha Moore Davis

Weathering Winter
A Gardener's Daybook
By Carl H. Klaus

The Wedding Dress
Stories from the Dakota Plains
By Carrie Young